MATT'S DILEMMA

THE WINSTONS SERIES

BOOK 2

ROWENA DAWN

SCARLET LEAF

2017

This is a work of fiction.

Names, characters, places and incidents are products of the author's imagination and are not to be construed as real. Any resemblance to actual events, locales, organizations or persons, living or dead, is entirely coincidental.

SCARLET LEAF

TORONTO ONTARIO CANADA

ISBN: 978-1-988397-96-2

For information address:

Scarlet Leaf:

scarletleafpublishinghouse@gmail.com

To Simona and Andrei

THE WINSTONS FAMILY

Rebecca's children

> Adam (m. Anna)

> Evelyne (deceased)

Adam's children

> Marjorie (Twin, m. Jonathan) – children: Matt (34), Maggie (28), Jay (28)

> Michael (Twin, m. Amelie) – children: Josh (26), Lily (26)

> Gabriel (m. Emilie) – children: Ariel (32), Alex (32), Becka (19; m. Bryan; twins: Lea and Sean)

8

CHAPTER ONE

"Becka, move your butt upstairs, now," Bryan's voice boomed and made Matt smile.

Matt knew Becka's policy of not locking the front door. He also knew Bryan didn't have much success in making her heed his advice.

That was why Matt didn't even bother knocking. He just came inside. After all, he felt there like at home. Becka and Bryan were some of the kindest in the family, although their couple was strange by far.

"I thought you liked my butt," Becka shouted from the study, and then stormed out of the room.

She missed Matt by an inch. She didn't even notice him and started taking the stairs two at a time.

"I love your butt, and you know it. But right now, bring it up here. She levitates, damn it, and she won't listen to me," Bryan's harangued voice came from somewhere above, and Matt burst into laughter.

Matt's imagination wasn't very strong, but at least, he guessed how stressed Bryan felt, having two gifted children.

As an outsider in the Winston family, Bryan had to put up with a lot of things. However, no one could say he shrunk his responsibilities.

Even if he didn't have a clue what to do in some circumstances, he dug his feet in the ground, and took everything in stride. Now, though, he seemed overwhelmed with his one-and-a-half-month daughter, who inherited her mother's family's heritage.

Only whispers came from upstairs, so Matt decided to go there, and visit with his niece and nephew. He knew his apparition would make Bryan roll his eyes. He'd understand Becka had failed to lock the door again, and he'd probably give her hell after Matt left.

He wouldn't say a thing in front of Matt. No matter how upset he was, Bryan never said anything to Becka in front of others. He thought they had judged her enough for marrying a man twelve years older, and she didn't need to hear any *'I told you'*.

Matt knocked on the nursery door, and Bryan looked up, concern edged on his face. When his eyes fell on Matt, his tension eased away, and he smiled, shaking his head.

"You haven't locked the front door again," he said in a resigned voice, glancing at Becka.

"I forgot," she shrugged, and patted his hand. "Don't worry, no one will come in, but Matt. Hi, Matt, what's up?"

Matt couldn't hide his amusement. His younger cousin was always a delight, and he enjoyed seeing Bryan struggle both with his concern for her, and his ineffectiveness in making her understand the dangers of the city.

"Just passing by. I've got an hour to kill and thought of coming and seeing you two. And the munchkins."

Matt came inside and went to Becka, who was holding Lea in her arms. He kissed Becka's cheek, and then, stroked the baby's head and put a kiss on the top of her head.

"She's already causing problems, I hear," he turned to Bryan, who raised an eyebrow inquiringly. "I heard you when I came in," Matt confessed, and a naughty smile appeared on his lips.

Becka blushed. She remembered what Bryan had shouted to make her come upstairs. She speared him with a pointed look, and Bryan just grinned.

Matt chuckled. He loved both of them and his heart burst with joy whenever he thought how good they were together. Yet, he was jealous of them sometimes, because he couldn't have the same thing.

"So, the problems started, I understand," he said, nodding to the little bundle in Becka's arms.

'Yep, and it scares me shitless, to tell you the truth. Thank God, Sean hasn't manifested any kind of powers yet," Bryan replied.

"He will... In time," Matt told him, putting a reassuring hand on his shoulder. "You'll manage, don't worry. You've never struck me as a man who can't handle everything."

Bryan scowled, but didn't reply. He glanced at Becka, ready to say something, but she shushed him, putting her finger to her mouth.

"She's asleep again," she whispered, and Bryan came to her to take his daughter and replace her in her crib.

Becka and Matt started to the door, expecting Bryan to follow. When Matt looked back, Bryan was still watching his daughter sleep, and his expression was priceless.

Matt had liked Bryan since the moment they met. Yet, once he got to know him, his respect and feelings for the man evolved.

Bryan was a devoted husband and father, and it crushed Matt to see that hulk of a man so deeply in love with his family.

Matt went downstairs after Becka and found her in her study. She was typing something at her computer, checking a pile of papers at her elbow.

"What are you doing?" he asked her.

"I have to finish an essay. Just two more lines, and I'm done," she replied, but didn't look at him.

Matt leaned on the doorjamb, crossing his ankles, and kept silent so she could finish her work. A minute later, Bryan came downstairs, as well, and waved Matt to come to the kitchen with him.

Even before stepping into the kitchen, the aroma of a beef stew reached his nostrils, and he inhaled with pleasure. His stomach growled and Bryan, who was close to him, chuckled.

"Ready for lunch?" he teased Matt.

"I suppose you cooked," Matt inquired in a dry voice.

"You suppose well," Bryan replied. "I wouldn't let Becka into the kitchen. She's a walking disaster," he shrugged, and, going to the stove, picked up a wooden spoon to stir the stew.

"Am I?" Becka bristled from behind Matt, and Bryan winced.

"Come on, sweetie, you know you can't boil an egg," Bryan replied, yet, there was no reproach in his voice. "And we're fine, aren't we? It's no need for you to cook when I can do it very well," he added.

He came to her, took her head in the cradle of his palms, and kissed her lips tenderly. Matt turned to look out of the window. The tender display touched a yarning in his heart, he thought he'd squashed long ago.

"Hungry everyone?" Bryan asked, turning off the stove and taking bowls out of a cupboard.

"I'll set the table," Becka intervened.

"What's there to set, baby?" Bryan wondered. "Just take a seat and I'll bring everything to the table."

"But I want to help," Becka retorted with annoyance.

Matt knew she didn't want him to think she wasn't doing anything around, but he knew better. Bryan didn't allow her to do much.

"You've had enough to do today, Becka," Bryan stroked the side of her face and kissed the tip of her nose. "You had to go to school – and forgot to lock the door, in the process," he thought to add, "and you worked on your paper for the last couple of hours..."

"Yes, and you cooked, cleaned and took care of the babies," she replied. "And in a couple of hours, you'll have to go to the dojo for your afternoon and evening classes, so..."

"I can do it, don't worry," Bryan waved her concern away, at the same time, leading her to the table and helping her to sit. "You're a new mom, and must rest as much as possible," he pointed out.

"I was a new mom a month and a half ago, Bryan. I'm perfectly fine now," she replied stubbornly.

"And that's how you have to remain," he pushed on her shoulder when she tried to stand up. "Come on, Becka, just sit. I can carry three bowls to the table myself," he said in a frustrated tone.

Becka just shrugged, but didn't try to stand up again. Matt, who always enjoyed their sparring immensely, watched her. She was biting her lower lip, annoyed with something.

"What's the problem, pumpkin?" he asked quietly.

"He won't let me do anything," she snapped. "As if I'm fragile."

"I never said you're fragile," Bryan's voice came from a few feet away.

Becka and Matt turned to him, and Matt immediately stood up to help Bryan to put the heavy tray on the table. He'd filled three bowls to the rim and sliced warm homemade bread.

"I can tell you, you cook as well as my mom," Matt sniffed the stew, and grumbled in satisfaction.

Becka smiled, proud of Bryan. Aunt Marjorie was the best cook she'd ever met, and Matt's praise meant something.

She dipped her spoon in the stew, and fidgeted a little in her seat, before carrying to her mouth.

"Out with it," Bryan said. "Something's bothering you," he asked, looking at her sideways.

Matt knew Becka couldn't even sneeze without Bryan getting concerned.

"Well, if you want to know," she started saying hesitantly, "I don't think it is right for you to do everything. It's already been a month and a half since I gave birth, so I am perfectly able to…"

Bryan stopped her, touching her hand.

"Don't worry about, Becka. You do more than enough. You have to wake up at night and breastfeed, and…"

"Huh!" she snorted inelegantly, and Matt had to hide his smile.

"Huh?" Bryan asked. "What does that mean?"

"Whenever I wake up, you wake up too, so don't try to sell me on that stuff," Becka shrugged.

"I might wake up, but I don't breastfeed," he retorted, miffed.

Matt couldn't hold it anymore and burst into laughter.

"You two are comical. The first couple I've seen quarrelling because the other is doing more," he shook his head.

"You eat and shut up," Becka snapped at him. "I'm serious, here. Yes, I breastfeed, and yes, I go to school. That's the sum of my accomplishments," she sulked.

"I wouldn't say that," Bryan murmured. "You keep me happy, Becka," he said, taking her hand, and squeezing it with tenderness. "And don't worry so much. Your mom will send Rosa's daughter here tomorrow. She'll clean and do the laundry, so I won't have much to do."

"Finally," Becka said relieved. "At least, you won't do those anymore."

Matt grinned. He knew Becka wouldn't accept Bryan's hard work for long. Now, at least, she knew there was someone else to take up the brunt of the housework, because Bryan would have never accepted her help.

It wasn't easy to hire help in their houses though. They needed to keep the family's secret and they couldn't hire just anyone.

Luckily, their hired help worked for them generation after generation. Rosa was Becka's parents' housekeeper and Uncle Michael's housekeeper's daughter.

"So, she'll start tomorrow?" Becka asked.

Bryan just nodded and spooned more stew. Matt knew he must have been exhausted. He'd started doing everything long before the birth of his children, and also kept his training schedule.

They savored the beef stew in silence for a few minutes, and then Becka looked at him inquiringly.

"What?" he asked.

"I was wondering if you had any news," she shrugged, and took another slice of bread.

"What kind of news are you expecting?" Matt asked and following her example, helped himself to another slice of bread.

Bryan did know what to do in the kitchen. He imagined Bryan knew what to do in almost every situation. His cousin by marriage was one of the most resourceful and talented men in the family.

"You know, Matt," Becka insisted. "It's May 19th already."

"And?" Matt asked with dismay.

He knew where the conversation was going and didn't like it. Only Bryan looked from one to the other with curiosity.

"In July, it's your birthday," Becka doggedly continued. "On 27th," she thought to specify.

"So?" Matt asked, feigning disinterest. "Are you planning a party for me or what?"

"Don't try to play games with me, Matt Winston," Becka snapped, and her small fist hit the table. Bryan's eyebrows shot up. "You know very well what I'm talking about."

Matt shook his head, scooped more stew and chewed.

"Not really," he replied. "I was thinking of taking a cruise or something, that's true. I haven't made my mind yet, though," he shrugged.

Becka stared at him with disbelief. Then, she took a breath, ready to launch herself in a lecture. Bryan touched her arm and calmed her.

"Matt," he said. "I see there's something the matter here and I really don't want Becka riled up. So what is it?"

"Why don't you ask her?" Matt asked stubbornly. "I don't know what she wants from me," he answered with indifference, and continued eating.

He didn't really regret coming to their house. He liked watching them interact and loved the little ones. Moreover, he always ate well in Bryan's kitchen.

"Okay, sweetheart, what is it?" Bryan asked her. He understood Matt wouldn't give in.

"He'll be thirty-five on July 27th," Becka pointed out.

"And?" Bryan insisted. He knew there must have been much more than Matt's birthday.

"He'll lose everything then."

"What will he lose?" Bryan asked again, feeling like he was pulling teeth.

"His powers, his trust fund…"

"Oh, I see, now. So that thing has a deadline," Bryan nodded when the truth dawned on him.

He turned to Matt and expected he'd say something. Yet, Matt just continued eating. He wasn't interested in expanding on that story.

"Come on, Matt," Becka said. "You still have a little over a month and a half."

That made him freeze with the spoon half way to the mouth. His stunned eyes locked on Becka. After a few seconds of deafening silence, he put the spoon back in his bowl and asked, "Are you for real?"

"Now, what?" she asked, throwing her hands in the air.

Bryan mused. Becka had a real talent for drama sometimes.

Matt pushed the bowl away with regret. He did want to eat that stew. A frown appeared between his eyebrows and he stared Becka down.

"I couldn't find a woman to love until now and you seriously think I could find one in a month and a half," he noticed. "Bryan, your wife has lost her mind. I'm really sorry for you," he said, turning to Bryan.

"Nah," Bryan replied. "Becka's smart and you should listen to her. It doesn't always take years to fall in love. It took me a day and a half, maybe less. And you still have over forty-five days, I think," Bryan shook his head, chastising him.

"Okay, I see it now. You're nauseatingly happy, both of you, and see everything through pink glasses," Matt concluded, and started to stand up.

"Maybe yes and maybe no," Bryan replied. "That doesn't mean you can't finish your stew. Both Becka and I," he said, with a meaningful look at Becka, "will refrain from talking about this matter anymore. Right, sweetie?" he asked her and reluctantly, she nodded.

Undecided, Matt looked from one at the other, and, in the end, his hunger won. He sat back on his chair and pulled the bowl back in front of him.

"So, how's your schedule these days?" Bryan asked. "You said you'd like to come by my dojo for some training," he observed.

"Not today, though," Matt said with regret. "I have a late meeting. An ugly divorce case," he specified. "Are you there tomorrow? In the morning, for instance? I have a couple of free hours then."

"Yes, I am. It's Becka's day off school and she'll be staying with the brats. See, sweetie, you do things, so don't complain anymore," he turned to her.

CHAPTER TWO

Tension filled the conference room, yet Matt didn't appear affected. He leaned back in his chair, his ankle over his knee, his papers forgotten on the table.

He never needed to refresh his memory. Files played the role of props for him. He used them to intimidate. He never checked them, either in a conference room or in court.

The man next to him, his client, Paul Willow, was a sleek man in his thirties. He didn't like him, but his partner, Joshua, had accepted his case and, with Joshua suddenly married and in an extended honeymoon, the case had fallen in Matt's hands.

Something didn't seem quite right with that Paul Willow, but his divorce case didn't present any difficulty for Matt. The facts didn't leave any loophole for the opposing council.

"So, let's recap here," he addressed to the opposing lawyer, Fred Rhoades. "Mrs. Willow signed a prenup before marriage. It is a straightforward document. We all agree with that. If she cheated, she'd get nothing. We have four men willing to testify that they slept with her on several occasions. They might not be outstanding citizens, but their bad reputations will make our case stronger. Plus, Mr. Willow is willing to pay for a DNA test to prove Mrs. Willow's son is not his," he said very matter-of-factly, and stopped to gauge their expressions.

The lawyer seemed annoyed and started cleaning his glasses. Her client, Nora Willow, soon to be Nora Barnes, had paled and the shadows under her eyes swallowed almost half her face.

Matt didn't feel any kind of pity for her. He couldn't stand cheaters and gold diggers, and, according to the file he had on the table, that woman was both.

Interesting though, although she'd paled and her fingers were shaking, she didn't flinch under his stern eyes. She returned his look squarely, as if she hadn't felt any remorse or shame.

"Now, we can go to court. We can't lose. Everything is cut and dry. Of course, by the end of the proceedings, we'll have your reputation in shreds, Mrs. Willow, and your son will find out the truth about his mother," he told her directly, his scorn obvious, both in his voice and eyes. "Or we can settle now," he turned to the other lawyer. "She gets nothing, as the prenup says. My client will not pay any alimony to his ex-wife and her child. But the child won't find what kind of woman you are," he concluded, his eyes returning to her. "So, what would it be?"

Matt's voice didn't raise, not even a notch, as if he'd just read dull instructions. He finished presenting the alternatives and waited patiently for their decision.

Rhoades tried to whisper something to his client, but the woman put up her hand and quieted him.

"I'll sign the agreement," she told Matt in a very calm voice.

Matt had never seen such a composed woman in a divorce case as the woman before him. She didn't react verbally to anything. She didn't attack or tried to push the guilt on her ex-husband's shoulders. The only sign she felt something was that tremor of her fingers.

"It's not like I'd have wanted a cent of his money anyway," she continued. "And it is true, his contribution to the house was much higher than mine, so, of course, I couldn't have asked for the house. I should ask for the money I invested in the house," she pointed out, and Matt became more focused on her.

No way she'd give up that money, if she knew she was entitled to it. His eyes narrowed, and he tried to use his mental abilities to read her, but he didn't succeed, and that puzzled him. His mental powers hadn't completely developed, but he still could read something here and there.

"What I want, though, and this is *not* negotiable," she warned in a steely voice, "is that he signs a document giving up any kind of parental rights. He stated my son isn't his. He must sign the papers," she concluded, and the inflexions of her voice warned Matt, she wouldn't budge on that score.

Matt lifted his left eyebrow, pensively. The woman had a lot of guts for a woman painted as a slut. She kept surprising him, and he didn't like it.

He turned slightly to his client with an inquiring look. The man just shrugged.

"I don't care about parenting the brat. You can prepare the documents, can't you?" he asked Matt.

Matt nodded briefly and stood up.

"I'll be back in a couple of minutes. May I hope you won't start fighting while I'm gone?" he asked.

The woman's behavior wasn't natural. She didn't reproach, accused or pleaded. He feared she'd explode while he was away.

Nora just nodded, and, completely disinterested in her future ex-husband or the lawyer next to her, she picked up her cell phone and started checking messages or emails. Matt shook his head imperceptibly. That woman befuddled him.

Then, he left the room to ask his paralegal to prepare the documents and bring them in the conference room.

He didn't dare to stay away for long. His instincts told him something was very wrong, and he wanted to avoid any kind of ugly events.

He returned to the conference room and silence greeted him. Only his client was drumming his fingers on the tabletop. Fred Rhoades was checking an agenda, and Nora was standing near the window, admiring the square at the back of the building.

She turned her head when he returned, but when he told them the documents would be ready soon, she preferred to remain near the window.

The following fifteen minutes felt like hours. Matt tried to make small talk with his fellow lawyer, but Rhoades's monosyllabic answers annoyed him.

His client started texting back and forth with someone, and seemed to have the time of his life. His soon to be ex-wife, didn't leave the window until his paralegal had come with the papers.

Then, she approached the table, took her reading glasses out of her handbag, and, after reading the documents carefully, dignified, she signed them.

When she finished, she collected her things silently, ready to leave.

"Mrs. Willow," Matt stopped her, but when he saw the mocking glitter in her eyes, he corrected himself, "I apologize, I wanted to say Ms. Barnes. My paralegal brought these papers for you. You have info about how to change your name and everything. As Mr. Willow renounced his parental rights, you can also change your son's name, if you want to," he specified.

"Do I have to?" she asked, and, for the first time, she sounded fearful.

"No, you don't have to," Matt answered softly.

"Thank you," Nora said and stretched her hand to him.

Matt shook her hand briefly. Her skin was freezing cold, but that didn't bother him. The brief electrical shock did. His eyes were focused on her face, and the surprise in her eyes told him she felt it as well.

Matt stepped back, bowed his head, and started gathering the files. The door clicked behind her, but he didn't even turn.

CHAPTER THREE

When his phone rang, he stopped under the overhang of the newsstand shop, a newspaper under his arm, and his umbrella in his left hand.

The weather channel had announced frequent rain showers and thunderstorms for that day, and he'd left the house prepared. They hadn't been wrong. It poured, and lightning lit the sky, covered with heavy clouds.

Matt took his cell phone out of his pocket and checked the screen. He frowned. Becka rarely called him so early in the morning, and he feared the worst. He'd seen her two days before and everything seemed fine.

"Hey, pumpkin, everything okay?" Matt asked Becka.

"I need your help," she said breathlessly, as if she'd run for her life.

"What happened?" Matt inquired, his heart beating frantically, and his fingers clenched on the umbrella handle.

The panic in his voice must have reached Becka's ears, because she hurried to say, "Oh, no, Matt, nothing happened. I've just run to take cover. It's pouring, you know. And I can't call you from home. I need your help to buy a gift for Bryan. Of course, I couldn't call when he could hear me," she chastised him.

Matt breathed relieved. He hadn't realized he was holding his breath.

"Thank God, Becka. You scared me," he confessed. "When do you want to buy that gift?"

"Are you free now? I'm in town, not far from your office," she replied.

"I'm not in the office. You know the shops across from my office? I'm there. I came to buy a newspaper and I was thinking to go for a coffee or something."

"Oh, Matt, it's perfect. Can you make it to the mall? I'm already there. Most of the shops will open in half an hour. We can have a snack together before that," Becka said with enthusiasm.

"Won't Bryan get upset if you eat now, and then, skip the lunch he cooked?" Matt asked her maliciously, his eyes wandering along the road.

"Nope. He'll cook dinner today, but not lunch. I'm supposed to have lunch at U of T, and he will be at his dojo. Mom came in the morning to spend time with the babies, until I get back at three," Becka explained.

"Okay, Becka, we have a deal. See you at Timmies, in about fifteen minutes, all right?" Matt gave in.

"Great, Matty. I knew you'd help me," she replied enthusiastically and disconnected the call.

Matt sighed and resigned to walk through the rain to the mall. He opened his umbrella, and started down the street, whistling a merry tune. At the traffic lights, he crossed to the other side of the road, so he could head right to the mall.

Few people passed by. Most people had found cover somewhere, so he could move at ease. Most of the time, that part of town was crowded.

Suddenly, the wind intensified and almost blew his umbrella away. He grabbed the handle better, and angled the umbrella against the rain pour, which came sideways now.

He pushed ahead mulishly, his head down, and mumbled to himself. Becka had chosen the wrong day to go shopping.

He heard an anguished cry and looked up. A few meters away, a woman with a toddler in her arms, was fighting the wind. Her umbrella had broken, and her bags had fallen to the ground. She shielded the child as much as she could, and now was trying to collect her things.

Matt rushed up and picked her bags fast. He started to hand them to her, and only then, he saw her face and practically froze.

Nora Barnes looked at him warily. The rain plastered her long red hair to her face, neck and shoulders. Her wet summer dress left little to imagination. It showed every single curve of her body and outlined her underwear. Her arms full of a fidgeting toddler, Nora tried to balance everything in the other hand.

"So, we meet again, Ms. Barnes," Matt drawled.

"Yes, it seems so," she replied in an indifferent voice, yet her eyes betrayed her nervousness.

She tried to take the bags from his hand, but he pulled them to him. She frowned. Her lips parted, and her entire face showed she was puzzled. His actions didn't make sense.

"What are you doing out with your child in this rain?" Matt inquired, his voice far from friendly. "This isn't the responsible action of a parent," he observed.

He closed the distance between them, so he could hold the umbrella above the toddler's head. Grudgingly, he protected her as well.

"Well, parents can't dictate the weather, Mr. Winston," she replied sarcastically. "And parents do need to go to work and leave children at a daycare, when there's no one to watch for them at home."

"Huh! I wouldn't have thought you'd get a job so soon," Matt said maliciously.

He didn't think that type of woman would look for work. Generally, someone like her would immediately look for another sucker to pay her bills.

"Not that's your business, but I've had this job for over seven years," Nora replied, peevishly.

She'd have preferred to keep her mouth shut and let him think whatever he wanted. Yet, she was afraid he'd consider she wasn't a good mother, and he had the means and power to make her lose her child.

Matt scowled. No way she'd had a job for the last seven years.

"I'm not one of your swains, Ms. Barnes, and I don't believe everything I'm told."

She just shrugged, and said, "That's your prerogative. I do apologize, Mr. Winston, but I do have to get Nathan to daycare. I have several things to do before my shift today, and I really cannot spend the entire day here in the street with you."

Long eyelashes shadowed her green eyes, and the raindrops hanging on them distracted him. The green of the pupils reminded him of the lush meadows he'd seen in Scotland a few years before.

"Mr. Winston," she repeated more forcefully, "We do have to go."

"Hmm, I apologize. I spaced there for a few seconds," he replied. "Where are you headed?"

"Just told you, daycare," she said through tight teeth.

Nora didn't understand what was going on with him, but she didn't have the time to ponder upon his bizarre reactions. She had too many things to do that day. She'd just cleared the appointment she had with Nathan's doctor.

"I got that," he snapped. "But where? What direction?"

"None of your business," she replied.

"I'm afraid it's my business, Ms. Barnes," he answered sternly, and his unnerving eyes disconcerted her.

Afraid, she pointed toward the entrance of the mall.

"We need to take the train."

"Good, I'll take you there," he said.

Without relinquishing her bags, he slid an arm around the two of them, and gathered them under his umbrella, to herd them to the entrance of the mall. A slight tremor crossed her body, and vibrated in his hand, which was also holding the umbrella over them.

Nora didn't protest, although she was very angry. She was angry because of the rain and because of him. She was angry because she was stupidly afraid he'd do something to take her son away.

"Why are you doing this?" she asked, frustrated.

"Because I can," he answered calmly, and when she stopped in her tracks shocked by his nonchalant answer, he just nudged her ahead.

***

When he arrived at Timmy's, Becka was seated at a table in the corner. She already had two cups of coffee on the table, and two breakfast sandwiches, so he didn't stop at the counter. The young woman seemed lost in her thoughts and didn't even notice his arrival.

"Hey, there, pumpkin. Why the long face?"

"What long face?" she smiled at him, standing up and giving him a warm hug. "I've got no reason for a long face. Just thinking," she assured him.

They attacked their sandwiches, and after the first bite, Becka started grilling him.

"Why did it take you so long to get here?"

He shrugged, "I met someone I knew, and we exchanged a few words, that's all."

"How come you're not wet?" Becka wondered, checking him out. "You don't have an umbrella. I got wet even with the umbrella," she observed, showing him the wet patches on her shirt.

"I had an umbrella, but I gave it to that someone," he waved her question away, as if not very important.

He'd foisted that umbrella on Nora. They'd fought back and forth for a few minutes for that darn umbrella, he remembered.

For such a small woman, she was very stubborn. In a way, she reminded him of Becka, but Becka had a sweetness, which Nora lacked.

Matt didn't know if it was the difference in their age, but the woman seemed hardened somehow. Becka would never be that way. With Bryan on her side, Becka would always keep her serenity and a certain innocence.

Becka sipped her coffee, her eyes on Matt, pensively. His dark hair, the shadow of his beard and his dark-blue eyes, as well as his impressive built, made him a favorite with the ladies. Yet, lately, he didn't even date. She had an idea why, but she hoped she was wrong. She didn't understand why Matt would sabotage himself.

"Are you all right, Matt?" she asked, touching his hand with hers.

"Yeah, why?" he looked up at her. For a moment there, he'd got lost in his thoughts.

"I don't know. It's something about you, you know. And you haven't even shaved…"

"Ah, that," he smiled, mischievously. "I don't have to meet clients today, pumpkin. So, I indulged. Don't read more into it than it is," he reassured her, patting her hand.

He finished his sandwich, drank his coffee almost in one go, and then asked her, "So, what about that present for Bryan? What's the occasion?"

"Ah, that," Becka said, starting to gather the wrappers. "On 23rd, it's Bryan's anniversary. I wanted to have a party for him, but he said no. I asked if I could invite at least a few of the cousins, and he said, sure, if I wanted the company, but not for his birthday. He doesn't seem comfortable with that. I think no one has ever celebrated his birthday, you know?" Becka said ruefully.

"Then, you could celebrate it with him. Just the two of you. A romantic evening, something to drink – oh, sorry, you can't drink, I forgot," he smiled at her remorsefully.

"I know, but I could just sip one drop of champagne, I think. Just to toast for him," she said, in an insecure voice.

"Yes, you could do that. It won't harm your babies or you, I am sure."

"And I want to buy a present for him. I was thinking of something practical, something he'd use, and something whimsical, just for the fun of it. But I don't want to buy a shirt or a tie," she shuddered. "Oh, gosh, imagine Bryan with a tie!"

Matt chuckled, although Becka was right. Bryan didn't wear a tie. Ever. He'd wanted to wear one for their wedding, but Becka had refused to have him uncomfortable that day. He was probably one of the few grooms who didn't wear a formal attire at a big wedding.

Matt thought a little, and then said, "I know what you could do for him. You could organize a small gym in the basement. In that room, next to the laundry. You can put a boxing bag, a treadmill, and a home gym – I saw one. It offers the possibility of thirty exercises. He'd be set for the days when he can't go to the dojo."

"You're a genius, Matty," Becka jumped off her chair and smacked a kiss on his cheek. "I was thinking on the same lines, but didn't know exactly what to do. You know I don't really have any experience with that," she admitted.

"Yep, I know," Matt grinned.

He remembered one of Becka's visits in his house, a couple of years ago. She wanted to try the treadmill. She simply fell and was almost thrown away. He had a hard time to explain her bruises to his uncle. For over half a year, he was forbidden to come to their house.

"I know where we should go to buy everything you'd need. Now, the problem is how we set everything up, without Bryan's knowledge, of course," Matt said.

"Well, if we hurry," Becka said, checking her watch, "we'd have about five hours per total. That means to do the shopping and arrange the gym. Would it be possible?" she asked, her wide, imploring eyes fixed on him.

"Yes, of course, we can do it. If we don't waste time looking for that whimsical thing you want to buy," he specified, standing up.

Becka waved her hand and then, she snatched the tray before Matt could take it.

"I'll take care of this, Matt. And no, I won't buy the whimsical thing today. I don't need advice for that, "she explained.

"Then, we can do it," he concluded and after she took care of the tray and wrappings, he took her hand to lead her to the shop he had in mind.

CHAPTER FOUR

When the alarm rang off, Matt woke up mumbling, then growled and stopped it with a violent slap. He sat up and rubbed his face, trying to dislodge the sand scratching his eyeballs. He ruffled his hair, running his fingers through it.

He glanced at the clock and scowled. He'd slept only three hours and the lack of sleep had left his brain in a dense fog.

He got out of bed and went to the bathroom, wondering where the days, when he didn't need more than an hour or two of sleep, had gone.

He leaned on the wash bowl and dared to glance at his reflection in the mirror. He regretted it at once. *Oh, man.* He almost didn't recognize the man staring back at him.

When, the heck, have I grown so old? Lines marred his forehead and black shadows outlined his eyes. His one-day stubble hid the civilized man, he liked to show to the world.

He shook his head in puzzlement. Not even six years ago, he could party all night, and then, go to the court the following day, his mind clear and focused on the case. Of course, he hadn't partied so hard ever since.

Pondering that mystery, he turned on the faucet, and picked up his toothbrush. Brushing his teeth, he thought he was fortunate enough that day. At least, he didn't have a court day that morning, and, if he remembered correctly – which could have been questionable, considering the blur in his mind, he didn't have any pressing appointments.

His eyes narrowed to slits. *Why, the heck, did I wake up? I could have slept a couple of hours more.*

Yesterday, Bryan had been so happy with Becka's present that he'd caved in, and accepted her party proposition. They hadn't invited many people, just Jay and Matt, and a couple of Bryan's friends.

Yet, they'd partied until four in the morning, and Matt got home and in bed only after four thirty, which accounted for his bloodshot eyes and the dryness of his mouth. The mirror didn't flatter him that morning, and his thirty-something body protested vocally to the lack of rest.

Matt remembered he used to feel that way only when he had a hangover. Yet, he knew he hadn't drunk anything else but a couple of beers and a glass of champagne the night before. He could drink a bit more without getting wasted.

Brushing his teeth refreshed his mood enough, so, he took a long shower, which made him feel almost whole again. He considered shaving, but pushed the thought to the back of his mind with disgust.

He didn't have anyone to impress, and didn't enjoy the thought of wasting ten minutes just for that. He could do with that beard for another day. *I heard beards are trendy again, so…*

His stomach protested and Matt opened the fridge, thinking he could use a sandwich or something. His eyes laid on a lonely tomato, forgotten on a shelf. *Worse than Sahara around here,* he scowled and slammed the door.

He didn't remember when he'd gone grocery shopping the last time. A quick search through the cupboards depressed him and made him grab his car keys, determined to head for the first Timmy he could find.

***

He'd been in the line for over fifteen minutes. The line moved slowly on, and the increased need for caffeine put a metallic shine in his eyes. With narrowed eyes, he willed the cashier to move faster.

Matt understood the guy was in training and had his own limitations, but he didn't understand the logic of using a trainee at peak hours.

What smart ass thought it would be good for business? A location to avoid in the future, he thought. He could find a Timmy not far from his office.

Everyone was irate. People were in a rush to get to work and lots of unpleasant comments flew around. The dissatisfaction escalated more and more, yet it didn't bother any of the employees milling around, without a specific purpose.

Matt's tiredness and hunger made him less charitable toward the young man, who moved with the lightning speed of a turtle. He still had two more customers before him, and started to jingle his car keys, impatiently.

After five more agonizing minutes, and a string of sweet words, addressed to the young employee mentally, Matt finally put his order in and got his coffee.

He moved to the side to wait for his sandwich, and relished the thought of tasting the black coffee, he'd waited for so long.

Matt had barely sipped from his coffee cup that the cell phone vibrated in his pocket. *What now?* he mumbled. They could have waited for him to enjoy that coffee first.

Resigned, he took the phone out of his pocket and checked the screen: St. Michael's Hospital. He frowned at first, and then, the implications hit him square in the chest. Someone close was hurt. He forgot about the coffee instantly.

"Hello, Matthew Winston speaking," his grave voice announced.

"Mr. Winston, I'm officer James Preston. Do you know a Nora Barnes, sir?"

Matt clenched his fingers on the phone. Yes, he knew Nora Barnes, but he didn't understand why the police would call him.

"Sir?" the officer's voice sounded inquiringly on the line.

"Yes, I know a Nora Barnes," Matt found his voice. "Why?" he asked.

"Would you be able to come to St. Michael's?" the officer avoided giving him a direct answer. "I'd be at the emergency room entrance," he specified.

Matt disliked the officer's underhanded manner, but couldn't refuse to go there. He had a bad feeling about the reason for that call.

"I should be there in maximum ten minutes," he confirmed and disconnected the call.

Matt was about to leave, forgetting about his sandwich, when his number got called. He shrugged, took his sandwich and coffee and left the coffee shop.

He hesitated in front of the shop for a moment, pondering the wisdom of taking his car from the parking lot. Then, he thought better.

I doubt there's any parking space there. Better I leave it here, he thought and went to add some more money for the parking.

***

Matt entered the hospital full of apprehension. He abhorred hospitals and made a habit not to visit any, if none of his family members was in there. Then, he didn't have a choice.

Officer Preston, a solid forty-something man, was waiting near the entrance, talking to the security guard. He'd probably made a joke because the guard was laughing loudly, with no respect for the sick people, waiting not even a few feet away from them.

"I'm Matthew Winston," he said, closing the space between him and the two men. "You called me," he said to the police officer, who was watching him as if he'd been an exotic exhibit. *It's probably the beard*, Matt thought.

"Oh, yes, Mr. Winston," the officer greeted him. "Let's go to that corner and talk without interference," he proposed pointing to one side of the waiting room.

Matt gritted his teeth. He wanted to hear why he was called and didn't give a fig if anyone had heard them.

"I understand you know Ms. Barnes," the officer stated.

"Yes, I do. I've already said so," Matt replied, his fingers clenching into fists.

He'd worked with police before, but that specific officer didn't have any consideration about wasting his time.

"You know she's a paramedic," the officer assumed, and Matt nodded.

He didn't know anything of the kind, of course. He hadn't been interested enough to check her background, but he wanted the officer to continue, and didn't think his denial would help.

"We were called to a scene this morning. The person who called said they needed the police, but also an ambulance, because people were hurt," the officer explained and rubbed his moustache. "Ms. Barnes and her colleague got there a few minutes before the police cars. The shooter hadn't left the scene yet, you see," the man continued, "and both of them were shot."

Matt's blood ran cold and he put his hands in his pockets. They were shaking, and he clenched his fists to control the tremor. His dark-blue eyes had turned metallic.

"Now," the officer continued, "Jack Nolan, Ms. Barnes's partner, wasn't hurt very bad. The bullet missed the artery. He was still conscious when we got to the scene, and was trying to get to Ms. Barnes. She wasn't so lucky," the police officer said flatly. "Two bullets in her chest, one in her left leg and one in her left arm. The shooter was furious because of a woman. That one had run away, so he took his anger out on Ms. Barnes," Preston said without inflexion.

Matt swallowed hard and brushed his forehead with unsteady fingers. He might not have liked Nora Barnes much, but only two days before, he'd seen her and she was fine. He couldn't imagine that young and composed woman, lying on a slab in the morgue.

"Has she died?" he managed to ask, through tightened teeth.

"No, don't worry yet. She's still alive. In surgery, but alive. They reserved the prognosis yet, but... Anyway, we spoke to Jake Nolan. And he mentioned two things. First, Ms. Barnes has a son," the officer said, counting on fingers.

"Yes, Nathan. He's about three," Matt replied in a hoarse voice, massaging the base of his nose.

"Yes, that's what Nolan said," Preston nodded in agreement. "Now, it seems Ms. Barnes is a valuable employee and has some leeway. She works some modified shifts, something like that. She'd arranged with her manager to leave at eight-thirty and take the kid to the daycare. She has a neighbour she pays to stay with the kid after she leaves at five thirty, but that woman must leave for work at nine fifteen or something like that," he said and looked at Matt meaningfully.

"I see," Matt replied, because the police officer seemed to expect an answer.

"Nolan says she has no one to help her out. In the past, she told him she must make it home in time because the neighbour was very clear she wouldn't wait. Nolan also says Ms. Barnes is adamant not to have the kid taken by social services, you see," Preston confided.

"Yes, I see," he replied dutifully, wondering where the man was going with all that prattle.

"We talked to Nolan, who, by the way, is with my partner right now," he thought to specify, and Matt just stared at him.

Why, the heck, would he think I'd be interested who's with Nolan? I don't even know that Nolan. Maybe one of Nora's conquests, he reflected with malice. He felt raw and mean, at the same time.

"Nolan implored us not to let the child go to social services, and the doctor said, if Ms. Barnes survived, it would be good if she didn't stress out, and this thing with the child would stress her, guaranteed," the officer nodded.

Matt kept staring at him. He didn't understand what the man wanted from him.

"So?" he asked, a migraine drumming in his temples.

"Nolan didn't know anyone close to Ms. Barnes. I understand her parents died. She's completely estranged from her ex-husband, who considered the child wasn't his, and didn't want to have anything to do with him."

"Yeah, so?" Matt asked more forcefully, his patience already at an end.

"Well, Nolan remembered she mentioned you, Matthew Winston, two days ago. He said she complained of your domineering demeanour and that you made her take your umbrella, and stuff like that. So, he thought you might be her boyfriend," the officer said and Matt's eyes widened in shock.

"We looked through her bag and found some papers with your letterhead and we called your office. They gave us your phone number, you see," the officer explained.

"Yes, I see," Matt said in a tired voice. "So, what do you want me to do?" he asked, in a matter-of-fact voice.

Yet, his heart cringed in his chest, and the air, suddenly, seemed in short supply.

"I knew we could count on you," Preston slapped him on the shoulder, and chuckled.

CHAPTER FIVE

This time, contrary to his custom, Matt didn't burst into Becka and Bryan's house. He didn't even think to check and see whether the door was locked or not. He was still in shock and he couldn't react normally. He pushed the bell, and waited patiently for someone to come and open the door.

His mind was in turmoil, and he couldn't focus on anything specific. His world had turned upside down in a matter of hours, and he could do nothing more but keep a façade of calm. He was far from being calm, though.

Bryan opened the door, a smile on his lips. His smile stopped when his eyes lay on the bundle Matt had in his arms. He could see only a mop of brown-reddish hair, sticking everywhere on the head of a toddler, whose face was hidden in Matt's shirt.

"Hey, there," Bryan greeted them in a soft voice and with a small smile, although he'd already noticed the storm brewing in Matt's eyes. "Would you like to come in?" he asked when Matt didn't answer.

Matt, unable to speak yet, nodded curtly and passed by Bryan into the house. Bryan shook his head, and then, closed the door behind him.

"Let's go out on the patio. We've decided on a brunch today," Bryan explained to him, just to fill in the silence. "Becka has no school and I took the morning and half of afternoon off," he continued.

Matt didn't seem to hear a word.

Bryan was aware of Matt's strange disposition, and he didn't want to push him. He'd always known Matt was very deep and his calm was a mere fabrication. He'd always believed Matt would explode one day, and he'd proposed himself to be far away when that would happen.

"Look who came to visit, Becka," Bryan told his wife in a cheerful voice, stopping next to Matt.

The toddler still held on Matt's neck and didn't dare to look around. Bryan saw the stuffed leg of a plush toy coming from between the child's body and Matt.

"Hi, Matt," Becka said softly, standing up and coming to him.

She touched his cheek, looked straight into his eyes and shook her head.

"Why don't you two take a seat?" she invited them. "And maybe you can introduce us to your little friend."

Matt nodded and sat down, the child always hanging on him. With a few whispers, he convinced the boy to sit in his lap and face his cousins.

"This is Nathan, Nat for short," Matt told them. "Nat, these are my cousins, Becka and

Bryan. They're fine, don't worry," he said, stroking the toddler's head.

"Would you like a cookie?" Becka asked Nat. "Bryan bakes the best cookies in the land," she continued cheerfully, and made the child smile shyly.

When she presented a plate with cookies to him, Nat chose carefully, and started nibbling on the chocolate cookie immediately.

"You'd like some milk, too," Bryan guessed, and poured milk in a cup, which he handed to Matt.

Matt took the cup, but froze for a moment. Bryan held his look, and gradually, he got to something close to his normal self, and helped Nat to drink some milk. When the boy pushed the cup away, Matt chuckled – a white mustache rimmed the child's upper lip.

"How old are you?" Becka asked Nat.

The boy considered her carefully, and then showed her three fingers.

"Oh, you're already three," she exclaimed cheerfully, again. "You're a big boy, not a baby," she said with exaggerated wonder.

Nat nodded seriously, and Matt stroked his head.

"Do you want some more milk?" he asked the child who'd finished the cookie already.

Nat shook his head, and then looked around.

"Would you like to run through the garden?" Matt asked. "It is okay, isn't it?" she asked Becka.

"Of course, it is," she said. "It's all yours, Nat," she invited him to take control of her savage garden.

The boy's face lit with delight, and he squirmed in Matt's lap to be let go. Matt lowered him to the ground, and he shot as fast as his short legs allowed him to the first bunch of colorful flowers. On his haunches, he touched the petals with awe, yet he never let the teddy-bear under his arm go.

"Should we talk now or…?" Becka asked Matt.

Matt shook his head, his eyes on the boy.

"He has to sleep soon, I think. Toddlers sleep during the day, don't they?" he asked turning to them.

Bryan smiled at him and shrugged, "Not something I'd know. I haven't had any experience with any other children, but my own. And they have a long way till they become toddlers."

"We can call aunt Marjorie or mother," Becka proposed, but Matt shook his head.

"No way. I don't want them to know anything right now. If later it's necessary, I'll tell them, but not now," he repeated stubbornly.

"Then we can check the Internet," Becka said.

"That's a good idea," Bryan said. "I'll bring the laptop," he announced, going inside.

Becka and Matt waited for him in silence. Nat was muttering something to a flower, but no one understood what he was saying. The regular breathing of the twins came through the monitor, Becka had put on the corner of the table earlier.

Bryan returned with the laptop and a notebook to take notes.

"I imagine you'd like to know more, not only if he sleeps during the day," Bryan explained the notebook. "We can make notes of what's important. It's a good lesson for Becka and me, as well."

Becka and Matt nodded and the three adults started their research about a toddler's timetable and routines, all the time glancing at the child, who had a lot of fun talking to the flowers and insects he found.

Half an hour later, Nat came to Matt and nudged him.

"Yes, pal, what is it?" Matt asked.

"You read," the boy said.

Matt seemed confused a few seconds, but Becka intervened.

"I think Nat wants you to read to him. That's what you want, Nat, yes?" she asked the child.

Nat nodded vigorously, stretching his arms to be taken up, and Matt sighed. He stood up, took him in his arms and told Becka and Bryan, "He asked me to take a few books with us. They're in the car. I'll be back in a moment."

"Don't trouble yourself," Bryan stopped him. Give me the keys, tell me where the books are, and I'll bring them."

"That's a much better idea," Matt agreed and handed the car keys to Bryan.

He sat back with Nat on his lap.

"Bryan will bring the books and you will choose one. But only one," he said in an authoritative voice, when a greedy light shone in the toddler's eyes.

His eyes focused on the child, when Becka's musical laughter reached his ears. He looked at her. She had fun on his expense.

"Becka!" he warned her.

"Come on, Matt, you're so funny. And I can see you'd be a good daddy," she added seriously, and Matt paled at her words.

"Don't even joke on that subject, Becka. It's forbidden topic," he argued.

"If you say so," she shrugged.

CHAPTER SIX

"He's finally asleep. Thanks, guys, for lending me that monitor," Matt said, pointing to the second monitor on the patio table.

"Don't sweat it," Bryan answered. "No big deal. We bought four to be sure we had one working if anything happened, so…"

"Anyway…" Matt started, but Becka stopped him, touching his hand.

"Forget about that, Matt, and spill the beans," she insisted, and Bryan smiled.

He liked it when Becka reacted with authority. Her attitude was in such a contrast with her small frame that it amused him to no end.

Matt explained about Nora and what happened that morning.

"I had to go and get the child. That woman didn't have a conscience, man. I got there exactly when she was coming out of the door. She didn't care she left the boy alone," Matt said, and his voice shook with anger. "And she did ask me to pay her for the time she stayed there. What kind of mother leaves a child with someone like her?"

"Maybe a mother who had no other choice," Bryan replied softly. "Did she mistreat the child?"

"No, but…"

"And probably Nora intended to be back on time," Becka reminded him. "I understand she arranged her shift so she could have plenty of time to go and get Nat, before that woman would have left."

"But she should have thought she could get hurt," Matt insisted mulishly. "With her type of job…"

"Not necessarily, Matt," Bryan disagreed. "It's not like she's in the line of fire all the time. Probably, it was the first time something like that happened, you know."

"I think," Becka said thoughtfully, "you resent her because of the way her ex-husband portrayed her during the divorce."

Matt stared at her for a few seconds, and shrugged.

"It was true, you know. She didn't fight back and didn't say he was lying about her being a serial cheater."

"Serial cheater? Really?" Becka asked and her eyes narrowed. "Why? Because her ex, who apparently has enough money to buy witnesses, says so?"

"She didn't defend herself, Becka," Matt replied in a very matter-of-fact voice.

"What would have been the point? Does she have money to fight you?" Bryan inquired in a quiet voice.

"I don't know," Matt admitted. "But she could have said something."

"If it had been pointless," Bryan shrug, "I understand why she didn't. Did you verify the facts yourself?"

"No, of course not. Everything was on file when it landed on my desk."

"Then," Becka said poking him with a finger, "you can't know what's true or not, so don't throw rocks, Matt. I thought you were more ethical than that," she reproached.

"But she didn't defend herself," he bellowed, "don't you get it?"

"You have to figure it for yourself," Bryan shook his head, and slapped him on the shoulder. "We can talk till we're blue in the face, Matt, but only you can uncover the truth. Anyway, what now?"

"I don't know," Matt admitted. "There's no one who can take care of the child. If child services take him, she'll face some serious problems to get him back," he said, and his face darkened.

"So?" Becka insisted.

"So… For the moment, I'm stuck with the kid. The problem is they live in a very small apartment. One bedroom, a tiny living-room and kitchen. The bathroom has a tiny shower. I wouldn't even fit in there... I was thinking to move him and his stuff in my apartment," he said pensively.

Becka approved, nodding. Bryan just smiled, enjoying Matt's thinking process.

"I could take care of him," Matt said not very convinced. "I mean, I have the time. We have cases on the roll now, but I have three young associates who could handle them... I can lend them a hand now and then, without effectively going to the office... I'd have to take time off, you know," he told them, glancing from one at the other. "I don't know where his daycare is so, that's out... I will have to go grocery shopping... This morning, I discovered I had only one tomato in my fridge, and half a box of cereals in a cupboard. Nothing else, not even a box of coffee or tea," he opened his arms in exasperation, and the other two smiled.

He paused, and a frown appeared between his eyebrows.

"I don't know how to do with the cooking though," he admitted. "And I don't want to involve my mom. Would it be bad if I buy fast-food?" he asked, and both Becka and Bryan nodded vigorously.

"Don't worry," Bryan said. "First, did you check their fridge?"

Matt closed his eyes with a scowl on his face, and slapped his forehead.

"I didn't even think of that. I should go and do it, I think. God knows how long she'll be in hospital. She wouldn't like to find living beings in her fridge when she comes back home."

"Definitely," Becka said, laughing.

"We'll go check it together, all right?" Bryan said. "And then, knowing what's there, I can start making some food for you. It's no big deal," he put his hand up when Matt wanted to interrupt him. "I'll make enough for two or three days. When you finish it, just let me know and I start a new batch."

"Oh, my God, how long do you think she'd be in hospital? If she survives, I mean, because it wasn't very clear she would," he clarified in a bleak tone.

"Don't worry, she will," Becka stroke his arm.

"The boy should sleep at least two more hours," Bryan said. "Let's go and take his things from that apartment and check the fridge. We'll go grocery shopping on the way back here. Becka can take care of him if he wakes up and Marissa's here, if Becka needs help. Is it all right with you?" he asked his wife.

"Sure," Becka said. "I'll manage, no worries. Just go," she pushed them out of her garden.

***

"Smart of you to mention that fridge," Matt told Bryan. "All those vegetables and fruit would have gone to waste."

"Told you. From what you said, Nora seems a very devoted mother, Matt. I don't know how you can't see it. Anyway, I was sure she'd have a lot of good food for the child. We need to buy only a few things for you – coffee, tea, things like that, and you're set for a few days. I'll make you a few casseroles for today and tomorrow, at least, and you can just warm them in the microwave."

Matt shook his head and said, "You can't imagine how grateful I am to you right now."

"Matt, you are a smart guy, who can also read minds. Read mine, already, and stop bothering me with your misplaced gratitude. We're family, man.

You were there for me when I needed you. I'm here for you now," Bryan said quietly, arranging the last things in the truck of his car.

He'd insisted on taking his car because he didn't like how shaken Matt was, and didn't want to risk him behind the wheel.

Matt, even shaken, decided to probe Bryan's mind. He avoided doing it, as a norm, because he didn't like to intrude in people's thoughts. Yet, he wasn't always successful in holding back. As he didn't have enough control of his gift, he picked random thoughts now and then, even if he didn't want to pry.

This time, though, he felt compelled to pry. Bryan's thoughts levelled him. The man really didn't think Matt should be grateful, and was willing to do everything in his power to help him.

The day had been a roller-coaster of emotions and shocks for Matt. The man tried hard to recollect himself when tears pricked at the back of his eyes.

He longed for his usual self, but it seemed more and more afar and difficult to reach.

The two men returned to Bryan's house just after Nat woke up. Tears welled in the little boy's eyes.

The thought Matt had also left scared him. He didn't understand why his mommy wasn't coming to take him, and he clung to Matt, as if he'd been his last resort.

"Come on, munchkin, let's eat a banana," Matt said, "and stop crying. I won't leave you. You won't get rid of me so soon. We'll go to my house to live until mommy comes home, all right."

"Mommy says no stranger," the boy replied, and looked at him with big eyes.

"I'm sure she did," Matt said, "and she's right, Nat, but I'm no stranger. You saw me talking to your mommy."

Nat rubbed his eyes and pondered over his words, then he nodded.

"Banana?" he asked.

"Yes, you'll have a banana," Matt confirmed and sat him on a stuffed pillow, he'd previously placed on one of the garden armchairs.

"Do you want me to slice it?" he asked Nat after he made sure the child was secure.

"I'm not a baby," Nat countered. "I can eat a banana," he added, and the mutinous expression in his eyes warmed Matt's heart.

He smiled and shook his head, "Yes, you're not a baby. Here you are," he handed the banana to him, and then watched him peeling it carefully.

The kid was focused on his task and didn't pay attention to them. Becka leaned toward Matt and whispered, "Have you noticed he doesn't talk like a small child?"

"Is that bad?" Matt straightened, with a glint in his eyes.

"No, don't be silly," she laughed. "He's just very intelligent. Someone took good care with his education. I'm sorry I have to point it out to you, Matt, but the woman you described wouldn't have done that. I do think you have to gather all the facts before judging her," she shook her head at him, disapprovingly.

Matt watched the child and thought Becka was right. His eyes turned pensive, and Bryan slapped him friendly over the shoulder, "You'll straighten everything up, I count on you."

Marissa came out with a fresh pot of coffee for the adults and filled their cups, making small talk with them. She left them with their coffees, and went inside, brushing her fingers through Nat's hair. Nat laughed.

"He's a very sociable child," Matt noticed. "I expected problems, you know. Especially because he saw me only once, and even then, I quarreled with his mother."

Bryan waved his hands, "All's good, Matt, you'll see."

He hadn't even finished reassuring Matt that Matt's cell phone rang. Taking it out of his pocket, Matt verified the screen and winced.

"What?" Becka asked.

"The hospital," Matt said, and took a few steps away from the child, so he couldn't hear what he was saying.

"Matthew Winston speaking," he said.

Both Becka and Bryan were focused on him. Matt paced, ran his fingers through his hair and then, pinched the base of his nose. He was frustrated and upset.

"I'll be there in half an hour, probably," he replied, and listened some more, nodding. "All right, I understand and, of course, I'll come," he added and turned off the phone.

"Guys, I have to go to the hospital. She's awake and frantic. She was told I have…" he said, pointing to Nat.

"Not a problem," Bryan said. "He can stay here until you come back, Matt."

Matt nodded and thanked him. Then, he knelt next to Nathan and told him, "I have to run an errand, Nat. You'll stay with Becka and Bryan here, and I'll be back in no time."

"No," the child said. "I won't stay. I come with you."

"I'm sorry, munchkin, but I can't take you in a hospital. I promise to be back. You'll have fun here. You can make cookies with Becka and…"

Bryan interjected immediately, "God forbid, Matt. Becka has red light in the kitchen. If Nat makes any cookies, it will be with me."

The alarm in Bryan's voice didn't sit well with Becka, "Come on, Bryan, is it really necessary to…"

Bryan stopped her with a finger on her lips, "Sweetie, you know it is. Imagine the fire alarm raging. The babies waking up… No, love, you won't touch anything in the kitchen. I thought we had an agreement," he said in a very serious voice, and Becka, reluctantly, agreed.

"Yes, Nat, you'll make cakes with Bryan, and afterwards, we'll draw something, okay?" she asked him.

The child stared Matt down.

"I promise to be back this afternoon," Matt repeated, seeing the mutinous expression of the child. "I won't leave you."

The boy considered him a few more seconds and then agreed with a nod. Matt hugged him, laughing, and turned to leave.

"Take a cab, Matt," Bryan suggested.

He feared the visit at the hospital would shake him. Matt had already had his share of shocks that day, and Bryan didn't think it was smart to let him drive.

"I'll call you one right now," he said and went inside.

Matt had to give in. Bryan's thoughts had been too loud for him not to hear. He understood the man's concern for him and he didn't want to repay his kindness with callousness.

CHAPTER SEVEN

The nurse buzzed him into the intensive care unit immediately after his arrival. Her stern and reproachful face made him uncomfortable, as if he'd been a teenager again, called to the principal's office for one of the pranks for which he'd been so famous.

"She's been frantic, but she refused a sedative. You need to calm her down. Her fever spiked, and that's not good," she explained to Matt.

Matt nodded and followed her to Nora's ICU room. He looked at her through the glass, before opening the door. The bed seemed to swallow her whole, and his heart cringed.

"Try to calm her down, not to agitate her," the nurse warned him again, in an authoritative voice.

"Of course," Matt replied, although he doubted he wouldn't agitate her.

The nurse left him there, and he gathered his courage to open the door. He knew his visit might cause her much more anguish and even though he didn't like her, he didn't want to cause her more problems than she had.

The moment he entered the room, she turned her head to him, and he felt the intense gaze of those green eyes right in his chest. She watched him with something akin to hatred.

He was only a few feet away, but even from that distance he noticed the tears clinging to her lashes. He felt the impulse to console her and balled his hands into fists to prevent any dumb move.

She looked paler than he remembered, even though the fever, which glimmered in her eyes, had flushed her cheekbones. The dark shadows under her eyes had expanded and swallowed almost half of her face.

Under his scrutiny, she made an effort to wipe the tears off her face, but one arm was hooked to the IV unit and she couldn't make use of the other, yet not for lack of trying.

She seemed determined, and afraid she'd hurt herself worse, Matt rushed to the bed, quieted her movements, and wiped off her tears with his thumbs. The gesture felt extremely intimate. Uncomfortable with that closeness, he hurried to step back.

She'd trembled under his touch, and his eyes searched her face to see whether she was afraid of him. The display of emotions didn't reassure him.

"I want my son back," she enunciated, and her voice was strong, far from the weakly form she presented.

"Don't worry about that right now," Matt replied quietly. "Just…"

"I want my son back," she almost shouted at him, interrupting him.

"As soon as you get out of the hospital you'll have your son back," he said, always patiently. "Right now, I don't see how you could keep him here with you," he waved his hand, showing the antiseptic hospital room.

"I won't let you take him away from me," she said, as if he'd never said anything.

Matt sighed, bowed his head resignedly, and ran his fingers through his hair. He needed patience with her, no matter what.

The nurse had already bad-mugged him, and he didn't want to be the recipient of her looks if he failed to reassure that woman.

"Look, Nora..." he began, but of course she interrupted again.

"I won't let you," she interrupted in a mulish voice. "You've attacked my dignity, insulted me in any possible way and made everything in your power to leave me penniless – and I'm talking about the money belonging to me, not to that sorry excuse of a human being that was my ex..."

Matt noticed she gathered more steam along her declaration, and the flush of her cheeks intensified. He worried her fever went up and decided to end that stupid sparring.

He stepped next to the bed and leaned over her. He hushed her with his hand, which covered half of her face. Her eyes widened, and again, he wondered whether he frightened her.

"Now, I want you to keep silent until I finish what I have to say. I don't want to hear one word from you, Nora," he warned her in a stern voice. "Do you understand?" he asked her.

He waited a couple of seconds, but she didn't answer. She just kept staring at him with those shimmering green eyes, which pierced him straight into his soul.

"I've asked if you understand," he repeat, sterner than before, trying not to think of what he felt.

After a second, she licked his palm, and he practically jumped out of his skin. He took his hand off her mouth immediately and watched her, shocked.

"You wanted an answer," she shrugged. "Well, with that shovel over my mouth, I couldn't have answered. So…" she explained, a quirky little smile in the corner of her mouth, and Matt had a glimpse of the naughty girl she must have been a few years back.

"But you'll keep your mouth shut and listen," he concluded, after taking a deep breath to calm his senses.

That lick had reached deep inside him, and all his nerve endings stood to attention. He didn't doubt she'd see the proof of his arousal if she looked closely, and he prayed she wouldn't. He'd have a hard time to explain that.

He tried to pry on her thoughts, but came back blank and that stunned him. He might not have had full ability, but still could read something from everyone.

"For the moment," she nodded slightly. "But make it fast," she warned him, and her eyes narrowed. "If I don't like what I hear, the entire hospital will know it, do you understand?" she finished in a menacing voice.

"Little girl," he smirked, "never make threats you can't carry on," he said, and tweaked the tip of her nose.

Nora huffed in indignation and opened her mouth to rebut him. Matt only touched a finger to her lips and shook his head, which made her keep quiet.

"Now, maybe I can speak in peace for a moment or two," he said. "So, that Nolan guy was concerned about the kid. By the way, you've found a *'great'* baby-sitter, Nora. When I got there, she was just getting out of the door and stopped just enough to ask for money. What kind of a woman leaves a small child alone in an apartment, huh?" he asked and a frown appeared between his eyebrows.

"I always..." Nora started, but Matt's finger was back on her lips to silence her.

"I'm talking now. And I wasn't talking about you. I imagined you'd have made it in time if the shooting hadn't happened. I wasn't accusing you. So, let me finish," he ordered.

"Where's my son now?" she asked, as if his finger hadn't touched her lips and he hadn't asked her to keep quiet.

Matt groaned, and bowed his head in mock resignation. He shook his head, and then looked back at her, a faint smile on his lips.

"You can't stop talking if your life depended on it, huh?"

"Where's my son?" she repeated doggedly. "I see you don't have him with you. Have you delivered him to child services?" she asked, and her voice shook. Now, fear was obvious in her voice.

"No, of course not. If I'd had that intention, I'd have let the police call child services in the morning and I'd have been done with it."

"So where is he?" she asked stubbornly.

"He's fine," Matt replied.

"Not what I asked," she retorted peevishly, and stared him down with a mean light in her eyes.

"Maybe not, but I thought to let you know he was fine. He's with Becka and Bryan," he replied.

"I don't know any Becka and Bryan," she observed and lifted an eyebrow interrogatively.

"They're my cousins," Matt answered. "At least, Becka's my cousin, and Bryan's her husband."

He took a few steps to the window to gather his thoughts. He had a few questions for her and didn't know how to ask them. He came back and observed her eyes had never left him.

"We couldn't determine if you knew someone who could take care of Nat. A relative or a friend..." he inquired mildly.

"I don't have relatives, at least not in Toronto," she admitted, and moved her fingers agitated. "I have a cousin and an aunt somewhere in BC... Friends..." she started to say and turned her eyes to the bed.

Matt waited a few moments, but she didn't continue.

"Yes, friends, Nora… Do you have any friends?"

She shook her head, and then looked up at him.

"Just a few people from work, but more like… acquaintances, you know… There's no time for friends… With work and a child…"

Matt noticed she avoided his eyes, and nudged her chin with his thumb. She looked at him, surprised, but he'd already seen she was uncomfortable admitting her loneliness to him.

"I understand things like that, Nora. You shouldn't be embarrassed."

A shadow crossed her face and she looked down again.

"What now?" he asked, turning her face back to him.

"It's not like you believe me anyway," she shrugged, and then hissed.

The movement of her shoulders had sent ripples of pain through her entire body, and she bit her lower lip not to yelp. Tears gathered in her eyes, turning their green in liquid intense glimmer.

"Calm, baby," Matt soothed her, tenderly stroking the side of her face.

Her puzzled eyes came back to him. Matt wasn't aware he'd used an endearment, but she'd felt his tenderness deep to the core.

"No unnecessary movements for a while, okay?" he told her and straightened.

Nora missed his touch immediately, and turned her eyes back to the utilitarian blanket, which was covering her up to midriff.

"I believe you don't have time to socialize," he reassured her, but noticed the ironic smirk appeared on her lips again. "What?"

"Mr. Winston," she drawled, "you thought I'm a femme fatale with a string of lovers to shame a call girl. I doubt that impression changed in the span of a few hours."

"My name's Matt," he replied in a sterner voice than he wanted, but her words had touched a sensible cord.

Bryan had sowed doubts in his mind about the file he was handed when asked to handle the Willows divorce. He was thinking of checking the facts again, although it was too late to do anything about the divorce.

"I think," she said hesitantly, "we lost the thread of conversation. You were telling me about my son…"

"Yes, let's get back to that," Matt conceded.

He wanted to return to safer ground. He didn't want to touch the matter of her divorce right then. He needed to find some answers first, and then he could either apologize or show her he wasn't a naïve young man.

"I took him with me," he said and put up his hand to stop her when she opened her mouth. "I'd have preferred not to take him from his environment, especially now, when he has to deal with your absence, as well. But I wouldn't have been able even to shower in your apartment. It's like a tiny doll house, for God's sake," he exclaimed. "We've spent the day with Becka and Bryan, as I've told you already, but we'll go back to my apartment tonight. Bryan helped me to gather Nat's things and empty the contents of your fridge," he told her and smiled. "I thought you wouldn't want to find it full of alien beings when you got back from hospital," he looked at her for confirmation.

"You thought well," she gave him his due.

"That's good," Matt grinned. "Anyway, we've done some research…"

"What research?" she narrowed her eyes.

"About toddlers, of course," he answered nonplussed. "It's not like I've been around many, and the two of them have only babies – twins, a month and a half old."

"Oh, my God, those people are so busy and you left my child in their hands…"

"As I said before, calm down, Nora," he snapped at her. "They're fine. Becka relates perfectly to children and Bryan is the embodiment of patience. Plus, Bryan will cook for us, enough for two days…"

"Bryan?" she asked, not sure she heard him correctly.

"Yes, why?" Matt looked at her inquiringly.

"Bryan will cook for you," she repeated to make sure she heard him.

"Yes, specifically for Nat. Our research showed fast food wasn't very good for him and I don't know to cook at all," Matt explained.

"But how come Bryan… Never mind…" she decided to drop the subject.

Matt finally understood why she was so astonished.

"I get it now," he laughed. "You wonder why Becka won't cook. It's simple. Bryan won't allow her to step in the kitchen… No, no, it's not like that," he rushed to explain when he saw her frown, "Becka's just a disaster waiting to happen in the kitchen. Even if she tries to boil an egg, freaky accidents happen. So, in their family, Bryan's the cook."

"Oh, he's a cook," she said relieved.

"No, he's not. He's a kick-boxing and Brazilian jiu-jitsu trainer," Matt said and, when her face fell comically, he grinned.

"You're pulling my leg," she accused.

"Nope, I'm telling you the truth," Matt shook his head. "Bryan is… a very interesting character, I'd say. I like him, you know… You'll like him too," he said quietly, and looked at her with a strange intensity, she felt down to her belly.

Matt kept quiet for a few seconds, and then, continued, "Look, I think we should do this. I won't bring Nat here," he said and, seeing she wanted to say something, he stopped her. "No, don't take it wrong. I won't bring him here, as long as you're in the ICU. I don't think you want him to see you like this," he said and looked at her inquiringly.

Nora shook her head, "Of course, not. He might not understand and he'd get upset."

"Exactly," Matt approved. "As soon as they move you into a reserve, I will bring him there to see you, all right?"

"I might get a semi-private room. I think my insurance covers that," she said thoughtfully.

"Don't think about that now," Matt waved her thoughts away.

He'd already decided to discuss the room matter with the hospital and cover a private room from his own pocket. He didn't want to bring Nat into a room with someone else he didn't know and might scare the child.

"Meanwhile, if you want, you could talk to Nat over the phone," he offered. "I think that would work for maximum two or three days, if you're good enough and get better," he grinned at her, and Nora scowled at him in response.

"It's not up to me, you loggerhead," she observed.

"Oh, yes, it is," Matt insisted. "It depends on your mind. You know, mind over matter," he explained.

"That's bullshit and you know it," she replied, crossly.

"No, actually, it isn't," Matt answered in a serious voice. "Your state of mind we'll help you recover sooner. Anyway, do you want to talk to Nat now or not?" he asked her, and tears welled in her eyes. "What now?" he asked with exasperation, opening his arms.

"Nothing, I'm just happy," Nora answered in a shaky voice. "So you won't take my son from me," she asked for reassurance.

"Don't be stupid," Matt's dry answer came, and he took out his phone and dialed Bryan's number.

He listened with half an ear to the conversation Nora had with her son. He was thinking how to organize everything and made mental notes to get in touch with his personal assistant that evening and rearrange his schedule for an entire month. Matt knew he had a few appointments he needed to keep, but hoped to get rid of everything else.

He was more interested in the conversation Nora had with Becka and Bryan. She surprised him by smiling a few times and even laughing heartily at something one of the two said.

When she finished her conversation, she handed him the phone back.

"Thank you, Matt. I won't ever forget that," she told him and her eyes shone with gratitude.

"No big deal," he replied with nonchalance, although he doubted he'd ever be at ease when she trained those eyes on him.

He couldn't understand how she could affect him when he didn't like or respect the woman.

"Does Nat have any allergies, something I need to know?" he asked her.

"No, no allergies. He's a very healthy kid," she smiled at him. "About the daycare… I know you could leave him there, but they won't give it back to you," she said with a brief hesitation and bit her lip. "Maybe, if I call tomorrow… and see what they need…"

"Don't bother with that," he waved her offer away. "Is it important for his development to go there?" he reconsidered.

"Not really… Well, he plays with other children…"

"But couldn't I take him to a park and have him play with children there?" Matt inquired, pushing his hands into his pants pockets.

"Yes, you could. But don't you need to go to work?" she asked him, and her voice showed her surprise.

"I'm the boss," he replied dryly. "I decide when and if I work," he explained. "I'll have to go to the office for some appointments, and I do have a couple of court appointments scheduled, but Becka and Bryan assured me they'd look after him when I can't, so don't worry about it," he continued, balancing on the balls of his feet.

They assessed each other in silence for a few seconds and then, Nora said, "I can't thank you enough, Matt."

"You don't have to," he replied, always in a dry voice. "Everything will be fine, and, no, you owe me nothing," he thought to add for good measure.

She looked at him with disbelief, and then huffed, "Yeah, sure. You rearrange your entire life around my kid and I don't owe you…"

"No, you don't," Matt repeated forcefully. "So, are we good now? Can you get back to sleep so you recover sooner?"

She closed her eyes, shook her head and said, "Yeah, why not?"

"Good, then I'll see you tomorrow," he hurried to say and left the room.

She looked after him aback. *That's one weird man, Nora. Something's not right with him.*

***

Matt left the hospital after he discussed the possibility of covering the costs for a private room, once Nora would be moved into a regular hospital room.

He made sure they understood he didn't want any kind of fuss about who paid the bill, and he persuaded them. He explained Nora was a proud woman, and it wouldn't do any good to her health to have her riled. He pointed out she'd be if they told her he covered the costs.

In a cab, going back to Becka and Bryan, he questioned his reasons for reacting the way he did. He was a rational man, and never did anything without weighing carefully the pros and cons.

This time, though, he didn't even stop to think. Something pushed him to do things he'd have refused if he'd given himself time to ponder about them. It wasn't about the money, of course. He was far from wanting any.

Yet, his behavior was beyond his comprehension. He couldn't even say he'd been bewitched because he had first-hand knowledge about that. He knew a witch when he saw one, and Nora wasn't it.

Now, the question remained: what was about Nora? He behaved uncharacteristically whenever he was near her.

What the heck? I've changed my life for her completely in one day, and willingly.

When he realized that, Matt froze.

CHAPTER EIGHT

Matt woke up with a little bundle of joy bouncing on his stomach. He liked sleeping on his back and enjoying his king size order-made bed. Almost 6.2 feet tall, Matt needed all the space he could get.

He rubbed his face with one hand and steadied the kid with the other. It had become routine already. Every single morning, during the last four days, he'd woken up with Nat jumping up and down on him, and he wondered if the child did the same thing with his mother.

Matt thought about the differences in size and muscles between Nora and him. He wondered how she fared after such an episode. She was just a slip of a woman, no match for the energetic bouncing of the child.

His training with Bryan had defined his abs some more and he was in great shape, but it still felt like a mule kicked him in his stomach.

"All right, munchkin," he said, "I see you're up already."

Nat nodded vigorously, and showed him all his milk teeth. All in all, Matt observed with satisfaction, Nat was a very balanced and happy kid. He took everything in stride and didn't get riled easily.

"What made you so happy this morning?" Matt asked, setting the child aside and getting out of the bed.

"You promised I can go to Becka," the child enunciated correctly, almost jumping on the bed. "She promised we go to the park. She promised you'll take me on the lake on Saturday. And I can see my mom today again," the child talked a mile a minute, and Matt smiled.

"I see Becka promised a lot at my expense," he joked, but when the child glared, he hurried to add, "Now, don't worry, will do everything she promised, okay?"

Nat smiled happily again and jumped out of bed. He followed Matt into the bathroom, and, like every other morning, Matt helped him to clean his teeth, wash his face and comb his hair.

Matt had already found out the kid liked to choose his own clothes and get dressed by himself, so after he had his shower, he went to the kitchen to prepare breakfast for both of them.

He had a long day before him, starting with leaving Nat to Becka, so he could go into work. He had a court appearance in less than two hours, and it wouldn't do to be late.

***

Somewhat tired, Matt came to take Nat from Becka a little after three. By that hour, Nat must have finished his nap and, now, he was probably ready to go.

Matt also hoped to get some lunch from Bryan because he hadn't had the time for a bite since morning, and his stomach had been grumbling since noon.

He didn't bother to ring the bell. He doubted Becka had locked the door after he left their house in the morning. He knew Bryan didn't have any plans to go out that day, so he couldn't have discovered his wife's forgetfulness.

He went directly into the house and for a second there, froze. His great-grandmother raised voice came from the back of the house. When she wanted, Rebecca's voice boomed in a way that would have made a drill sergeant proud.

"I can't accept it, young man," she bellowed.

Matt immediately rushed through the kitchen and out onto the patio. It wasn't a stretch to think Rebecca was chastising Nat, and he couldn't allow it. The child was in his care and he wouldn't have permitted anyone to shout at him.

Rebecca wasn't a mean and unfeeling woman, but she did like to have her way every single time. Yet, this time, Matt couldn't let her.

Once outside in the garden, he stopped suddenly. Stunned, he stared at the scene before his eyes, and for a moment he was sure he hallucinated.

Rebecca held Nat in her lap, one arm around his midriff, and she pointed a bony finger to Bryan, who was sitting in a lawn armchair not far from her. Bryan tried to keep a serious face, but a stubborn smile fought to appear in the corner of his mouth.

"What's going on?" Matt asked in a voice far from mild.

Nat immediately turned to him and shouted, "Matt."

He held his arms up, so Matt could take him in his arms. Matt realized he'd become the child's anchor since his mother's shooting, and, curious enough, he didn't mind it. He actually enjoyed the pure joy on the kid's face whenever he saw him.

"Hush, now, young man," Rebecca told him with authority. "First, you must finish eating your snack, and then, you can go to Matt."

Obedient, Nat immediately snatched another biscuit off the plate on the table and stuffed it in his mouth. Everyone smiled, and Matt ruffled the boy's hair.

"Where's Becka?" he inquired, glancing at Bryan.

His great-grandmother waved her hand, "She's in the study. She had to take her mother's call," she explained.

"You see," Bryan intervened maliciously, crossing his arms over his chest with nonchalance, and stretching his legs in front of him, "Rebecca thought a double-front attack would be in order. Becka's mother would nag her, while Rebecca would bellow me into submission."

"Submission for what?" Matt asked. He hadn't heard any problems or complaints related to his favorite couple lately.

"For taking the trust money, of course," Rebecca snapped at him. "I've waited long enough. I've hoped they'd come to their senses sooner or later, but it's been almost a year. I won't take his refusal for an answer," she ended with obstinacy, and pointed the same bony finger to Bryan.

"Sweet great-grandma," he began but she interrupted him with a smirk.

"Don't take me with *sweet great-grandma*," she retorted. "I know you don't mean it and I won't have it."

"Don't mean it?" Bryan inquired with puzzlement.

"Of course, you don't mean it," she huffed. "I've seen you. I know how you think. You hate me and that's why you won't let Becka have the money," she explained in a bitter voice.

"Now, there, you're wrong. I do think you are sweet in your own way," Bryan replied.

When he saw she intended to contradict him, he stood up and put a hand on her shoulder.

"You don't show it, Rebecca, but you're not as mean as you want people to believe. About the money, sorry," he said and shook his head, "but I don't need it and Becka doesn't want it, that's all. Don't take it personally. I won't say I'm sorry she doesn't," he shook his head and patted her shoulder, as if he'd wanted to sweeten the blow.

He thought a moment and leaned over her and kissed her parchment-like cheek, which stunned her. Then, he started back to the house, throwing over the shoulder, "I suppose you're hungry, Matt. I'll bring you something, just take a seat."

Pleased, Matt smiled and sat next to Rebecca. Bryan was always considerate, and if he'd told someone how domestic Bryan had become, no one would have believed him.

Matt shook his head, amused, when he felt Rebecca's eyes on him. He turned to her and met her assessing sharp eyes.

"How have you been, grandma?" he politely asked her.

He had to do some conversation with her. He couldn't ignore her forever.

"Don't grandma me, Matt," she retorted. "You've got some explaining to do, young man," she said, looking at him pointedly.

Matt shook his head, and said quietly, "No, I don't have to explain anything."

"I care to differ and the proof is in my lap," she snapped, and Nat looked up at her.

"Me?" he inquired shyly, and Matt wanted to yell at his great-grandmother for not considering the child's feelings.

It wasn't something new for Rebecca, but he still hoped. At least, her age should have mollified her enough.

"You're the proof, kiddo, but in a good sense," she ruffled the boy's hair. "Now, finish eating if you want to play," she ordered in a voice that didn't allow any more inquiries.

Nat immediately snatched a slice of orange and shovelled it into his mouth. Satisfied, Rebecca smiled at him and stroked his head.

"So, when were you going to tell me you had a son?" she brusquely asked Matt.

Matt just stared at her. He'd have liked to answer something, anything, but his mind went blank in shock.

"You're my daddy," Nat said in awe, and the adoration in his voice humbled Matt.

The glimmer in the child's eyes shook Matt and he came back to reality.

"Thanks, grandma," he said sarcastically. "How can I now…" he started but couldn't finish.

"You take care of him, you're his dad. I don't care who fathered him," Rebecca replied and shrugged, as if everything had been very simple.

"You're my daddy," the child repeated, and Matt groaned.

"Should I congratulate you?" Bryan's dry voice came from behind him.

Matt looked up and saw the stern expression on Bryan's face. He didn't need his mind reading gift to know what his friend thought.

He raised his arms helplessly and asked, "What should I do, now?"

"It's not for me to know," Bryan replied curtly, and set a tray with a bowl of soup and a sandwich before him.

"What kind of question is that, Matt?" Rebecca huffed, and lowered the child to the ground. "Now, you can go and play," she told Nat and slapped his behind jokingly, making him laugh.

However, Nat didn't leave immediately. He looked at Matt and said, "You promised I can see mommy today."

"Of course, you will," Rebecca answered at once. "We'll all see mommy today."

Matt chocked, and soup gushed out of his mouth. Bryan jumped back, but Rebecca wasn't so lucky. She was right on the path of the liquid, and both her face and her top took the brunt of the spray.

"Matthew Winston!" she shouted, throwing her arms in the air, exasperated.

She hadn't expected something like that from Matt, not in million years. Matt had proved the most balanced of her grandchildren and great-grandchildren by far.

Nat and Bryan started laughing like hyenas, but Rebecca gave them the evil eye, huffing. She needn't do more, because they smothered their hilarity at once.

Nat chose to run to Becka's flowers, which fascinated him, and where Bryan had set up his outdoor toys, while Bryan gathered napkins to help Rebecca clean up.

Matt just stared at her. His eyes had widened. He couldn't believe he'd sprayed his fastidious great-grandma. But then, he couldn't believe her gumption. She just invited herself somewhere she had no business to go, and he'd be damned if he'd just rolled with it.

Rebecca huffed again and snatched the napkins from Bryan. She started wiping her face vigorously, still frowning.

All the time she made use of the napkins, she muttered, "I've never… never… never thought you'd do that to me… How, the heck, am I going out now? Huh?" she ended her muttering, with a shout from the top of her lungs, and she bad-mugged Matt again.

Matt still couldn't say a thing. His tongue was in knots. He'd have liked to say a lot of things, but none was appropriate for his great-grandma's ears.

Bryan intervened immediately. He noticed Rebecca was ready to slap Matt silly. Although he'd liked to see how it would go, considering that Matt was much taller than his great-grandma and outweighed her by at least 80 pounds, he didn't think the show would have been good for the kid.

"I'm sure you can borrow something from Becka," Bryan tried to soothe her, in a quiet voice. "It isn't the end of the world, you know? I know, you are taller, it's true, but she's rounder and it will compensate," he explained.

"Are you saying I look like a scarecrow, young man?" she changed her target suddenly, and rallied against Bryan, gathering more steam.

"Far from me, Rebecca," Bryan replied.

His voice was always calm. He didn't need another shouting match that day. Rebecca had given him enough grief that afternoon.

"Then are you saying Becka is too round?" she snapped at him, ready to defend her great-granddaughter.

"She's perfectly round," Bryan observed very matter-of-factly, "so, let's not get into an argument here."

"I think I should go," Matt finally found his voice.

He thought he'd take advantage of the sparring match between Rebecca and Bryan and sulk away with Nat. Yet, he thought wrong.

Rebecca immediately turned to him and barked, "Eat your lunch and keep your mouth shut. Maybe, this time, you can eat your soup without spraying me again."

Matt's worry escalated. He thought he knew Rebecca, but he didn't understand her game now. He only knew he'd have had a serious fight on his hands if he'd wanted to make her remain there, at Becka's house, or go home, but not to the hospital with him.

"Grandma," he started, but she didn't have any of it.

"I said, have your lunch," she snapped more forcefully. "You'll have enough time to talk to me this afternoon and evening," she observed.

Her words had the effect of a cold shower for Matt and strengthened his resolve.

"What do you mean?" he asked in a dry voice, pushing the tray away, definitely not hungry anymore.

"I decided to borrow a top from Becka, so you won't get rid of me so easily, Matt," she scowled at him. "I'll be ready in no time at all."

Matt frowned at Bryan because he was the one who'd had the idea to offer one of Becka's blouses. Bryan just shrugged, disinterested in Matt's anger.

"This is your battle, Matt," Bryan said.

"What battle?" Becka's voice came from behind him, and he turned his head to her.

He smiled at his wife and informed her, "Rebecca needs one of your tops, sweetie. Matt showered her with soup," he grinned.

Rebecca slapped his arm, unamused with his antics.

"Try to find one that goes with my skirt," she ordered Becka. "How did it go with your mom?" she asked slyly.

"We had a nice conversation, grandma, and no, I didn't accept the trust money," she said. "How come Matt sprayed you with the soup?" she asked, sitting in her husband's lap with fluidity.

"Don't change the subject, young lady," Rebecca snapped at her. "I want you to reconsider," she slapped her palm on the tabletop, vexed that the young woman hadn't bent down.

"Sorry, grandma, I can't," she shrugged, and her voice showed no contrition. "If you hadn't conditioned that money, things might have been different," she observed.

"You know why I did it," Rebeca defended her decision.

"I know and I understand your reasons, truly," Becka replied, and leaning forward, stroked her grandma's arm. "But that doesn't mean I agree with you. The way you treated Bryan..."

"Sweetie," Bryan intervened, but Becka hushed him, with a shake of her head and a finger firmly put on his lips.

"What did you expect me to do, when I saw a man like him with you?" Rebecca countered, waving her hand in Bryan's direction.

"A man like him?" Becka jumped off Bryan's lap, ready to do battle, and the air vibrated all around them.

Becka controlled her fury now, and things stopped flying around all the time. Yet, the air still vibrated whenever she grew angry, and her husband knew he had to do something.

Bryan attempted to intervene and pull her back in his lap, but she slapped his hands away.

"No, Bryan, she won't get away with insulting you once more," Becka said ferociously. "Once it was more than enough," she observed, and her eyes thundered to her great-grandma.

"But I didn't insult him, Becka, don't be stupid," the old woman said in a very unemotional voice, which contrasted with Becka's white fury. "I just said he's so imposing and serious and... I couldn't see you with a man like him... At that time," she thought to add when Becka practically growled. "I thought he'd stifle your exuberance and youth. Now, I know better," she shrugged. "You don't have to get in a huff, young lady. People, make mistakes. Just wait until you get to my age. Then, tell me you haven't made any," she challenged Becka.

Becka didn't have the time to answer because Matt chose that moment to stand. He braced his palms on the table, and reclaimed Rebecca's attention.

"I want to know what you plan to do," he demanded with authority and watched his grandma with steely eyes. "You've played enough with me already," he raised his voice.

He slapped the table top, finally losing his temper, and making a few eyebrows raise. Matt never showed if he was rattled or furious, and his outburst was uncharacteristic enough to astonish them.

'Now, I'm starting behaving like a loony bin', he thought, his eyes always fixed on the old woman. He knew she plotted something, and he didn't like the direction of her actions.

If he could have gone back to the early hours of the morning, he'd have made different plans for Nat that day. He'd have never taken the chance of letting Rebecca know what was going on.

"I'm planning to see your young lady, Matt," Rebecca said very straightforward, unimpressed with his temper. "With or without you," she pointed out.

Matt's eyes flashed with anger. He even had to step back so he wouldn't be tempted to knot his fingers around the old bird's neck.

"There's no such thing like *my young lady*, grandma," Matt said squarely, unwilling to attract Nat's attention.

"Who are you kidding, Matt?" Rebecca mocked him, waving her fingers to him. "Humph! No man takes over the care of a child just out of the kindness of his heart," she waved the assumption away, with a flutter of her hand.

"There was no one else, that's all," Matt groused.

"Sheesh!" Rebecca puffed. "You have enough money to pay someone, Matty. You are a kind man, I'll give you that, but kindness only goes so far. So, I want to meet the woman who…"

"You won't meet anyone," he snapped, interrupting her in a rude voice. "You'll stay here or go home, whatever you want, but you won't interfere in my business. Is it clear?" he practically growled at her.

"I don't like your tone," the old woman straightened her back and looked him down.

"I don't care," he answered. "You don't know when to stop. You tried to control everyone's life from the beginning, and it simply killed you that you couldn't control mine. Well, I don't care," his fist made contact with the tabletop. "I won't have it," he thundered to the old woman. "You can do whatever you want, great-grandma, but do it as far as possible from me and my business," he said in an icy voice now, aware he'd lost his temper and made a show of himself.

Then, he turned to Nat and stretched his hand toward the boy, "Nat, we're leaving to see your mom, now. Come on, munchkin."

Nat ran to him, forgetting about the yard toys he was playing with. Matt had bought him a crabbie sand table three days ago and Becka and Bryan had set it next to the flowerbed the child liked most.

"You promised Becka and Bryan can come too," he took Matt's hand.

"I know, but they have guests. They'll come with us tomorrow," Matt smiled and ruffled the child's hair.

"No, need," Rebecca intervened. "We can all go with you now. I just have to change my top, Nat, and we'll be on our way."

She'd already understood Matt didn't want to say anything wrong before the child and she took advantage of his weakness. She knew how to play her hand and succeed in her plans.

She didn't have any notion of pity. Sometimes, people needed a steely back to survive, and she had learned early not to show kindness when she shouldn't, and not to back down when she wanted something.

This time, Matt effectively saw red. He let go to Nat's hand and turned to Rebecca. His expression showed he was now ready to say everything he wished to say, no holds barred.

Becka whispered fearfully, "Bryan, do something."

CHAPTER NINE

Bryan's intervention spared both Matt and Rebecca of a total fallout. Matt left their house with the kid and Becka in tow, and Bryan remained to deal with the old witch, as Matt was thinking of her now.

Matt rarely had bad thoughts about his great-grandma. He understood why her heart had grown cold and why she wanted to control everything and everyone, even though he didn't like it.

They'd butted heads over the years, sometimes more, sometimes less. The worse had been when he brought Velma with him to introduce her to the family. Yet, even then, Rebecca hadn't made him see red, ready to lash out at her and spit out all the resentments he'd gathered over the years.

This time she hadn't just stepped over boundaries, she'd blown them up completely.

Matt was more furious because she'd made all those comments in front of the child. If the child had repeated any of them to his mother, which was a strong possibility, Nora would have been convinced Matt wanted to steal her child from her.

And just like that, they'd be back to square one. Over the last few days, they'd found a common ground somehow. Nora was less circumspect and fearful of him, and a few barriers had come down, which he loved.

When they moved her into a reserve, he'd brought Nat to visit. The child had helped their interactions and she'd opened more to Matt.

The glimmer of resentment and hatred had disappeared from her eyes, which relieved him. That now she was also well on her way to recovery added to his satisfaction.

He'd told himself he was satisfied they'd part ways soon, but he knew he was lying to himself.

There was something there, although he wasn't sure what. He'd never been so muddled in the head when it came to a relation with a woman. He didn't know whether he wanted to see more of her in the future or not.

Their conversations had become less strained, and he'd learned she was an interesting woman, far from the materialistic and cheating female he'd thought her before.

He still couldn't glimpse into her mind. He didn't belabor over his inability to read her thoughts and took everything in stride.

He'd discovered things about her in the same way a regular person with no paranormal power learned about the people around, and that seemed to be more satisfying than just reading someone's mind.

He'd also hired an investigator to dig into her past and her ex's past and present. He couldn't forget what Bryan had told him and he wanted to see whether he'd been duped.

It saddened him to hear she'd been on her own for most of her life. Her parents had moved to Florida when she was barely eighteen. They died there, in a break-in, a few years later.

The investigator researched the divorce evidence and came back empty. He'd established beyond any doubt that it was impossible for the four witnesses to have had an affair with her. Not only had they never met her, but at the times of the alleged dates, Nora was always working.

What he found was evidence against the ex-husband, though. Apparently, he'd had two girlfriends on the side and for some time already.

Matt had sworn never to accept a file again without checking the evidence himself. He knew Nora had been doled a terrible injustice and he'd been the instrument of her humiliation. Whenever he remembered how he'd talked to her, he gnashed his teeth in frustration.

"Are you alright, Matt?" Becka touched his arm.

He glanced at her for a second and then checked the child in the back seat.

"Yes, I'm fine. Just a little raw after… Well, after, you know."

Becka just nodded and glanced out of the window.

"You know, I don't think anyone has ever stood against her and that's why she thinks she can do everything she wants," she remarked pensively.

"I don't give a... fig," Matt censored his language, both for Becka and Nat's sake. He felt raw and mean and needed to swear. "I've had enough with her meddling and her demands," he slapped his hand on the driving wheel.

"I know. But... she's old... and... in her way, she does love all of us. As a matter of fact, everyone knows she loves you more than anyone else," she pointed out to him.

"Like I care," he shrugged, a scowl etched on his face. "I'd prefer she didn't love me at all."

"I like her," Nat's voice came from the back of the car, and Matt's eyebrows climbed on his forehead.

"Really? How come?" he asked the boy.

"She barks. She doesn't bite," Nat replied.

"Where did you hear that?" Matt asked him, surprised the boy could say something like that.

"Mom says so... About dad..."

"Your dad shouted as well?" Becka asked, turning in her seat to look at Nat.

"At mom," the child said. "He doesn't see me."

"How the... how come he doesn't see you?" Matt asked with disbelief, editing his words again.

"He says... I don't exist," the boy explained, and both Becka and Matt snarled.

"Maybe you didn't hear correctly," Becka tried to console him.

"No," Nat replied. "He said so. Many times."

"Bastard," Matt grumbled. "Someone should teach him a lesson. With their fists."

Becka heard him and smiled. Matt had always been willing to protect the underdog and dole the necessary punishment.

"Mommy needs flowers," Nat suddenly said.

"I bag your pardon?" Matt asked surprised, stopping at the traffic lights.

"Flowers. She needs flowers," the child insisted.

"How do you know?" Becka asked.

"Yesterday, I saw people with flowers. People bring flowers in a hospital," Nat repeated stubbornly.

"Okay, don't get your pants into a twist, pal," Matt laughed. "We'll buy flowers, buddy. Right there," he said, pointing to a flower shop. Then, he signaled to the right and changed lanes.

***

As Matt had allowed Nat to choose what flowers he liked, they made their entrance in Nora's room with a big basket. To Becka's delight, the toddler had chosen a basket full of Alstroemeria, which signify devotion, prosperity and fortune.

Nora's eyes widened when they fell on the basket, which supposedly Matt and Nat carried. Matt had convinced the boy they should both carry the basket. He doubted the boy had had the strength to hold it in his tiny hands.

She accepted the flowers gracefully, although she shook her head to Matt, chastising him for spending so much. She'd seen such baskets while window shopping and knew they were over $150. She couldn't believe the man would spend so much money just to humor a child.

Only then, she saw Becka. Her eyes had been riveted on Nat and Matt and almost missed the short, blond woman next to Matt. For a second, her heart cringed, but she chased away any sadness and smiled widely at Matt's companion.

"I'm Becka," she said, "Matt's cousin. I bear fruits," she showed a bag, where she'd stuffed a few oranges, bananas and apples. "Just stuff you can eat without the need of cutlery," she specified and placed the bag on the night stand next to Nora's bad.

"Becka's my friend, mom," Nat boasted. "She plays with me every day. She let me touch her babies. They're funny. No hair or almost no hair. And they sleep all the time or they cry," he rushed to say, tripping over his own words.

The adults smiled indulgently, and then, Nora turned to Becka.

"You can't imagine how grateful I'm to you for all the help…"

Becka interrupted her by touching her arm and shaking her head.

"You don't need to be grateful. It's good experience for my husband and me. My babies won't be babies forever, you know," she laughed.

Nora nodded and laughed, as well, "Don't I know it! It's like now they're in the crib, just sleeping and asking for food every few hours, and, suddenly, you have a small typhoon on your hands."

"Should we put the flowers on that stand there?" Matt asked, suddenly unwilling to be left out of the conversation.

"Yes, I think it's perfect there," Nora replied, a strange shyness in her voice.

Matt's left eyebrow went up his forehead. He'd never seen her shy.

Nora invited them to sit. She had two chairs in the room and she took Nat on the bed with her. She kept touching him and brushing his hair, a sign she'd missed him terribly.

"So, you're good with Becka, Nat, yes?" she asked the little boy.

"Yes, and with Bryan. And I met their great-grandma today. And she is funny," the boy announced with exuberance.

Both Becka and Matt looked at him as if he'd lost his mind. There were lots of things one could say about Rebecca. Being funny wasn't one of her traits, though.

"What?" Nora asked, noticing their puzzlement.

"Great-grandma is anything but funny," Matt replied in a dry voice. "Not even when I was of Nat's age I thought differently," he explained.

Becka just nodded. She agreed wholeheartedly with everything Matt said.

Feeling Nora's inquiring eyes on her, she explained, "Great-grandma is… let's say, special. And she's good to take in very small doses. Today, both Matt and I had a little too much of her presence," she laughed.

Matt just growled and ruffled his hair with his nervous fingers.

"She said Matt's my dad," Nat announced proudly, jumping on the bed.

All three adults froze. Matt looked at him with widened eyes, Becka covered her mouth – she didn't know if she wanted to scream or laugh, and Nora watched Matt in shock.

"What did she say?" Nora asked in a small voice, afraid she'd hear the same thing again.

"Matt is my dad," Nat repeated, nodding vigorously. "And I agree," he let them know there was no doubt in his mind about Matt's identity.

"Say something, darn it," Nora snapped at Matt.

He shrugged, "I am at a loss of words."

"How can you be at a loss of words?" she rebuked him. "You're a lawyer, for God's sake. You don't do anything but talk all day long."

He scowled at her and groused, "That's what you think lawyers do all day? And what the heck do you want me to tell him? He's three. What will he understand?"

"I don't know," she threw her hands in the air, "but you need to say something, and soon," she pointed out.

"Why me and not you?" he retorted furiously. By now, his eyes glinted and he spoke through tight teeth.

When Nora didn't have anything to say, Becka intervened, "If you two don't mind, maybe it's better to leave it like this for the moment. There's enough time to…"

"When? After he's convinced Matt's his father?" Nora pounced on her.

"Hey, I'm not the enemy here," Becka thought to mention and put her hands up. "Yet, Matt still has to take care of Nat for a while and I don't think antagonizing..."

"He's my father," Nat interrupted her furious. "Great-grandma said so," he said, and everyone noticed tears in his eyes.

"No one says differently, kiddo," Becka replied, ruffling his hair. "Just adult talk," she laughed.

"Becka," Nora said, staring at Matt. "Would you mind taking Nat with you to the coffee shop downstairs and buy me a latte or something? I'd owe you one."

"Buy one for me too," Matt said taking money out of his pocket. "And Nat, they have cookies, I hear. See what you want."

"I have money, Matt Winston," Nora tried to push his hand away so Becka couldn't take his money.

"And so do I," Becka said and exhaled loudly. Then, she took Nat's hand and pulled him with her. "We'll buy you some cookies and me some white chocolate," she explained to him.

"I want white chocolate too," the child scowled.

"Then you shall have it," Becka laughed. "Nothing wrong with that, once in a blue mood," she told him in a conspiratorial voice and left the room.

Nora looked after them. Matt didn't need to be a mind reader to know she was furious.

"Look," he started, but she stopped him, shaking her head.

"You need to straighten things up. When they come back," she insisted.

"You're right, but your timing sucks," he explained and she glared at him.

"I know you're upset, but the child must live with me for at least another week if not a little more. I won't have him upset. In time, he might transfer his wish of having a father upon someone else or... I don't know, okay? I know, though, I can't upset him now. It's enough he misses you, don't you think?" he tried to soothe her, stroking her arm, but she jerked away, and he tightened his teeth in frustration.

"Yes, but when I get out and he won't see you, he'll think it's my fault, and I have to live with him for much longer time than you do," she said and poked him in his chest with a finger.

"Is it absolutely necessary that he doesn't see me anymore?" he asked her.

His question came like a blow and stunned her. Nora just looked at him.

The silence stretched for almost a minute. Matt ran his fingers through his hair agitated, and then said sarcastically, "I see you glow with glee at my proposition."

She shook her head, and replied, "You just... stunned me. I thought you couldn't wait to get rid of me and Nat."

"Nat is great," Matt pointed out. "Why would I want to get rid of him?"

"Me, then," she groused, hurt by his words.

"I've never said that. I… like you… I think," he shrugged. "I thought… we should try at least… I mean… we should see how it works… if it works… We haven't seen each other in the best light until now, you know. We might be surprised with what might be…" he continued wishfully, and his eyes swept over her.

The day when she moved into the private room, he'd brought her a set of sweats at her request. They hang loose on her, but didn't hide much of her shape.

Nora's eyes glimmered, taking him in. Then, she closed her eyes for a couple of seconds, clenched and unclenched her hands a few times, and then looked straight into his eyes.

"Right now, I have a phobia about any kind of relations with a man."

"I know you've just divorced and I don't want to pressure you…"

Matt took a step toward her, but she stopped his words and his advancement with a gesture.

"It's not the divorce, Matt. The divorce was the end. It's been about a few years of resentments and upset… and… I know I'm unfair right now, but I lump all men in the same category – unworthy, untrusty, and better gone from my life."

"I see," Matt said quietly. "I think… I won't bother you then. Once you've recovered and can take care of Nat, I'll remove myself from your life, don't worry," he replied bitterly.

Nora watched him carefully, and then came to him and touched his chest, "No, I don't think I truly want that. Maybe… we can try and see how it goes… But you know Nat goes where I go… I don't have anyone to leave him with and…"

"Don't worry," Matt replied, taking her hands in his. Hope glimmered in his eyes and his tone didn't have the same resigned and bitter sound. "I don't mind having Nat around. And maybe, now and then, he can stay with Becka and Bryan for a couple of hours, to give you some respite," he smiled at her.

"Definitely," came Becka's reply from the door.

They turned to her, both surprised, and not a little guilty, and Becka smirked.

"I think it is a great idea, Matt, and I am sure Nat thinks the same, don't you Nat? Don't you like spending time with me and Bryan?"

Nat nodded vigorously, and then said, "And Bryan even cooks. Like you, mom. His food is very good," he said and licked his lips, making them laugh.

"So, you're a good cook," Becka concluded. "That's just perfect. Matt can't cook anything," she shrugged. "A lot like me. Matt, do you think it's a gene missing in our genetic code or what?"

Matt chuckled, and nudged her chin with his thumb, "Oh, kiddo, you're so funny."

"By the way," Becka told Nora, "on Saturday, Matt will take Nat sailing."

Nora frowned and turned to Matt, "I don't think it's safe."

"Oh, yes, it is," Becka contradicted her and patted her on the shoulder to smother any upset. "Matt is the best and most careful sailor you'll find, plus he insists on guests wearing the life saving vests, so Nat will be in no danger."

Nora seemed a little reluctant, but the imploring face of her son made her turn to Matt, "Are you sure you can take care of him while sailing?"

"Of course, I can," he responded, offended by her lack of faith.

"And if I can convince my mom to take care of the babies, Bryan and I can accompany them," Becka chimed in.

"And we'll come to you in the afternoon, so you'll see Nat is in one piece," Matt joked, which he regretted immediately when Nora scowled at him.

"By the way," Becka said, "I am sorry, but tomorrow, Nat won't be able to come to visit. I bought tickets to a puppet show and it's exactly after his nap," she apologized. "I hoped you wouldn't mind..."

Nora shook her head, immediately, "No, it isn't a problem. I can survive without visitors for one day," she smiled, but her smile was sad.

"You'll still have me," Matt rushed to say.

Becka burst into laughter at the look on his face when he realized what he'd said.

"I mean, I'll still come," he rephrased his statement, bad-mugging Becka.

CHAPTER TEN

Matt couldn't wait to have a visit with Nora just for himself. He'd enjoyed watching her interacting with Nat, and he'd been very pleased to see Nora getting along with Becka.

However, he longed to be alone with her. He wanted to further the relationship he'd told her about, and that wasn't going quite smooth when there were witnesses in the room.

He drove and left Nat and Becka at the puppet show, promising he'd be back for them before it ended. He hurried to the hospital afterwards and, on the way there, he stopped to buy her a potted orchid.

He remembered Nat's words. People brought flowers when they came to visit someone in the hospital.

Matt thought a little further ahead, and decided to buy her some cookies to nibble on, a couple of magazines and a new book. He'd already brought her a couple of books the day before, but he didn't think she had too much to do in that hospital room. He'd have crawled on the walls, had he been in her place.

He wasn't very sure about the magazines, but he decided he couldn't go wrong with a National Geographic and a Reader's Digest.

***

A knock on the room's door brought a smile on Nora's lips. Matt was early, but she wasn't sorry he was there already.

She'd been thinking about that visit since the day before. Once he'd planted the idea in her head, she'd been thinking of nothing else.

She left the book she was reading on her pillow, and said, "Come in."

The door opened and, to her surprise, it wasn't Matt the one coming into the room. An old woman, well in her eighties if not older, entered her room with the gait of a general. Her white hair rendered her black eyes more compelling, and those eyes zeroed in on Nora, as soon as she entered and closed the door behind.

Although she could see some resemblance with Matt, especially in the way the woman carried herself and the shape of her eyes, nose and mouth, Nora remarked, "I'm afraid you have the wrong room."

The woman gave her the chills. Her piercing look and the smile perched on her lips didn't reassure Nora at all.

"I've got the right room," the woman said and advanced into the room. "I'm Rebecca, Matt's great-grandmother. I think it's high time we met," she observed stretching her hand to Nora.

Nora politely shook her hand, but replied, "I haven't even thought it was the time to meet each other. I'm just a passing acquaintance of Matt and…"

"Balderdash," Rebecca retorted, and Nora's eyes widened. "Passing acquaintance, my foot. My great-grandson doesn't make a habit of caring for people's children. I don't even think he'd spent more than a couple of minutes with a child before meeting you," she waved her hand dismissively.

"Probably, he had his reasons," Nora said softly, and indicated a chair to the old woman to sit down, even though she'd have preferred to send her on her merry way.

Rebecca sat on the chair while Nora perched on the edge of the mattress. Rebecca's visit made her anxious and her nervousness increased with every second.

Nora supposed the old woman had come to tell her *'shoo away and leave my great-grandson alone'*, and she wasn't sure how she should react.

She'd pondered everything carefully since the previous afternoon and felt she wanted to get to know Matt better. She didn't welcome Rebecca's interference but, for the moment, she decided to wait before reacting.

"I brought you some chocolates," Rebecca said, and took a box of chocolates out of her huge handbag.

Nora thanked her with half a voice and put the chocolates on the night stand, next to the flowers she'd received from Nat and Matt.

Both women assessed each other in silence for a couple of minutes, and then, Rebecca began her attack.

"So, you're the woman who bewitched my Matt," she said, and her voice implied she'd already judged Nora and found her wanting.

A warning light shone in Nora's eyes. She proposed to herself to be polite with the woman – she was old, after all, and Matt's great-grandma, but she wasn't willing to let her humiliate her.

She knew she was somewhat average. Her hair was just a touch too fiery, her skin extremely pale and her green eyes too prominent on her face because of the paleness. Even her height was average, barely 5.4. What wasn't so average was the roundness of her hips and thighs and the size of her bust.

"I must say I was dying of curiosity to meet you," Rebecca continued, not bothered with Nora's attempt to warn her off. "Matt has never been unkind, but he's never gone so out of the way to please someone. He'd arranged his personal and professional life around you and your son," she noticed.

"Let's leave my son alone," Nora asked in a mild voice, yet the underlying steel was there, and Rebecca chuckled.

"Let's not," she retorted and Nora's eyes flashed with storms. "I like the little imp. He's smart and energetic – a good child. Someone took good care of him," she gave Nora her due. "Anyways," she fluttered her hand, "the idea is there's something with you and you reeled my Matty in," the old woman continued.

Nora looked at her with disbelief. Yes, Matt showed some interest, but he didn't seem hooked on her. He just expressed some interest in exploring a possible relationship. That didn't mean he was bewitched, as Rebecca claimed.

"Don't look at me like that, young lady," Rebecca snapped. "I know my boy and I know he's infatuated with you."

"If he's just infatuated, you don't have anything to worry about," Nora remarked very matter-of-factly.

She was sitting, her back ramrod straight and her hands quiet in her lap. Yet, inside, she seethed.

How dare you come here and judge me? What makes you think you're above me?

"I'll worry if I want. Now, I want what's best for my boy," Rebecca continued, as if she'd discussed the weather. "You're good, probably, given how Nat turned out, but..." she paused for effect, "you're not the best."

For a second, Nora couldn't breathe. She knew the old bat would say that, and yet it surprised her.

"Why are you here again?" she asked with nonchalance, as if she hadn't been insulted already.

"It's very simple girl," Rebecca replied. "You need money. That's no doubt there," she continued, and irony sounded in her voice. "I already know everything about you. That's how I traced you here," she waved her hand, showing the hospital room. "Now, you need to tell me how much you'd need to let Matt go. His future is somewhere else," the woman concluded in a demanding voice.

Nora looked at her in shock. She'd expected a dress down, more insults, threats, possibly. She didn't expect a demand to name her price.

She needed only a few seconds to recover, though, and then, she jumped off the bed and started bellowing.

CHAPTER ELEVEN

An icy fog claimed Matt's mind when the nurse told him Nora had an older woman visiting with her. He knew who that woman might be.

He needed a few seconds to react, and gather his thoughts. Then, in a hurry, he threw a *'thank you'* to the nurse over his shoulder, and practically ran to Nora's hospital room.

He perceived a raised voice coming from the room just before opening the door. He didn't waste time with knocking, but threw the door open. He stopped in the threshold, his nostrils flaring and his eyebrows almost knotted in a terrible frown.

Nora was looming over his great-grandma, and he couldn't stop admiring how good she looked in warrior mode.

"Is it clear?" she continued, without noticing his arrival. "I don't need your money or your approval. You can shove both where..."

"Young lady," Rebecca stopped her. "Your language is deteriorating," she observed with an icy contempt.

"So what?" she replied back. "I don't care for your opinion about me and you cannot buy me."

"Of course, not," the old woman remarked. "It's not like you'd accept less when you know Matt's financial worth now. You wouldn't, would you?" she sneered.

"I don't need his money or yours," Nora stressed out. "I make what I need. What I want is for you to get out of here and never come back," she shouted.

Then, she turned to the door to open it and throw the old bat out. She went cold all over when her eyes fell on Matt.

He was watching her with impenetrable eyes. He looked good, although slightly harassed, and regret nested in her heart.

She was a practical woman, though, so she squashed any regrets and feelings, and said, "You're just in time to show your great-grandmother to the door. I'll ask for a discharge tomorrow morning, so, yes, I apologize, but I do need you to watch Nat for me tonight. Tomorrow, though, I'll take him out of your hands." By the end, her voice shook, although she had started calm enough.

Matt didn't answer at first. Her flat voice sounded strained to his ears. He looked into her eyes and found them dull. The light he'd seen there yesterday was gone.

"Yes, I'll show great-grandma to the door, and yes, if you want to leave the hospital and it's safe to do so, I'm all for it. What won't happen is to make me go away," he pointed out.

Closing the distance between them, he touched her faintly rosy-colored cheek with his fingers. Anger had powdered her skin and her lips were trembling.

Without thinking, he leaned down, and lightly touched his mouth to hers. His fingers lingered on her face for a few more moments, and then, he straightened.

He stared at her a little more, and then, handed her the bag with the things he'd brought her, "Hold onto this, Nora. I have to take care of my great-grandma," he mentioned sarcastically.

He turned to Rebecca and asked, mildly interested, "Are you going out on your own steam or do you need my help?"

Both women gasped. Nora couldn't believe her ears. She'd actually thought he'd leave and that would be the end of it.

Rebecca was even more stunned. She'd never imagined Matt would actually take action against her. He'd grumble, yes, but, in time, he'd resign to her way of thinking.

She'd tried to wedge a rift between Nora and Matt the day before, when she told the child Matt was his dad. She liked the boy well enough, but she didn't think Matt should be with someone just because of his sense of duty. She wanted something more for him.

"How dare you talk to me like that?" she pounced on him.

"I asked whether you leave by yourself or I needed to have you removed," he rephrased his previous statement and stared Rebecca down.

The old woman huffed, and the color raised in her face. Nora felt sorry for her when she saw her lips quiver.

"Matt," she touched his arm hesitantly. "Maybe you shouldn't..."

"I should have long ago," Matt contradicted her in a steely voice. "Excuse me, honey," he said, and moved her hand from his arm.

He stepped closer to Rebecca and, unnervingly, he asked her again, "So what'll be, great-grandma?"

"If you think Marjorie won't hear about this..." Rebecca threatened, but Matt put up his hand and stopped her.

"I don't give a... fig," he blue-pencilled his language. "Mother will understand," he shrugged. "Now, I want you to leave," he said in an even sterner voice.

Rebecca had had enough. She straightened and in the most authoritative voice, replied, "You understand you'd never get your hands on the trust money."

Nora gasped lightly. She hadn't intended to make Matt lose his money or put him in the cross hairs with his family because of her.

She rushed and touched his arm again, "Matt, I don't want you to..."

"But I do," he replied, always watching Rebecca with flinty eyes.

Rebecca realized he wouldn't back down, and she glared at him. She turned on her heels without a word and left the room.

Matt made note of her glare and knew what she'd do first. He turned to Nora, caressed her face with his fingers, and said, "I'm sorry, but I need to let mom know that Rebecca will park on her doorstep."

"Oh, my God, your mom will hate me, if only for that," Nora cried out with dismay.

Her chances with Matt became thinner and thinner, and she admonished herself for not listening to her reason.

She knew she shouldn't have gotten involved with anyone. She had other priorities in mind and again, she'd set herself up for disappointment.

"Be serious," Matt replied. "Mom's not like that," he explained to her and helped her sit on the bed.

Then, he took the phone out of his pocket to call his mother. He intended to call Jay afterward and ask him to go and take Becka and Nat from the theatre and bring them to the hospital.

CHAPTER TWELVE

Nora watched Matt talking to his brother, Jay, over the phone, and envied the easy camaraderie between the two. She'd never had such an open and warm relationship with anyone in her family.

The conversation with his brother relaxed Matt. He'd been enraged before.

She'd felt his tension – the man was hopping mad, and all that made her nervous. Now, though, he slowly came back to something close to his normal peaceful self.

Matt had surprised Nora a second time that day when he called his mother in her presence. She'd assumed he'd leave the room so she couldn't hear his explanations.

The call hadn't lasted long. Matt had succinctly explained to his mother that he had a girlfriend, which stunned Nora even more. She hadn't known he was thinking of her in those terms. Not that she minded. She might have been a realistic woman, but still liked to dream now and then, and she'd fantasized about Matt a lot, and in a very short span of time.

He'd also confessed to his mother that his choice didn't meet his great-grandma's expectations and, consequently, she had done her best to sabotage him, which he couldn't abide.

He hadn't gone into details, but warned her that Rebecca was probably on her way to her house. She'd definitely want to complain about the ungrateful brat, he'd turned out to be.

Nora hadn't been able to hear his mother's replies, but Matt's words and behavior had astonished her. He'd even chuckled a couple of times and in the end, he'd resignedly accepted an invitation to dinner on Nora's behalf for when she would leave the hospital.

Jay needed much less explanations than Matt's mother. Matt just told him he'd quarreled with Rebecca, who'd interfered in his relationship with Nora, and asked him to go and take Becka and Nat from the theatre and drive them to the hospital.

He didn't want to leave the hospital before he had a chance to speak to Nora, and Bryan was watching the babies that afternoon.

When he'd organized everything to his liking, he shoved the phone into his pocket and turned to her.

"I think I need to apologize for my great-grandma's behavior," Matt said, and his posture showed he wasn't very sure about what to say.

Nora had been standing all that time, and now, exhausted after all the commotion and the roller-coaster of emotions and thoughts, she walked with difficulty toward the bed and sat down. Her stiff and painful legs barely supported her.

The doctor had advised her to use crutches, but if she limped, she didn't put much weight on the injured leg. She preferred not to be encumbered by the crutches, especially because her chest hurt whenever she tried to use them.

She looked at him thoughtfully and replied, "You know she thinks I refused her money only because I thought you'd have more."

"And why would you care?" he asked her. "You didn't seem so concerned with what people thought of you a few days ago," he alluded to the day in his office.

"I didn't care about what you thought then," she admitted with a shrug, "but I seem to care now."

"And why do you care now?" Matt closed the distance between them.

He sat on the bed next to her and took her hand in his. He felt the light shake in her fingers.

'She's not indifferent to me. Far for it.' A satisfied smile perched on his lips and he squeezed her fingers carefully.

"Because it matters," Nora replied quietly, staring into his eyes. "It's impossible for you not to think I'm a fortune hunter, especially with everything you know about me," she continued ruefully.

She remembered very well what had been said in that conference room in his office. She didn't forget what he told her when they met in the street, either.

"I know better now," he said, and brought her fingers to his mouth.

Nora glared at him and reclaimed her fingers, "What do you know better now?"

Matt heaved a deep sigh. He knew he'd have to tell her one day, but he'd hoped that wouldn't be the day.

There had been enough turmoil for an afternoon, and he was afraid she wouldn't respond well when she found out the truth.

He needed emotional distance to do it, so he stood and sauntered to the window where he leaned on the windowsill. His eyes roamed over her, a strange light shining in his dark-blue pupils. He lingered over some choice spots, and his nostrils flared. Then, he turned serious and looked straight into her eyes.

"I've done what I should have done before you'd signed those divorce papers," he finally confessed.

She drew a long breath. She felt like she couldn't get enough air. She couldn't look away from him. Matt's eyes were very compelling.

"What does that mean?" she asked for clarifications.

"It means I hired an investigator," he replied quietly, watching her carefully. He didn't want to miss any of the reactions playing openly on her face.

"What for?" she flashed out at him, and her eyes narrowed.

She had some suspicions and she didn't like them at all. After finding out that Rebecca had checked on her, hearing the same thing from Matt made her seethe.

"Because, during the last few days, I got to know the real you, and what I read in that file before that meeting didn't match what lay before my eyes," he shrugged, to excuse himself.

"So, you wanted to make sure I didn't try to dupe you," she replied in a quarrelsome voice.

Matt didn't say anything for a few seconds and just looked at her. He just knew that what he was going to say might spoil his chances with her.

"Wouldn't you have done the same?" he asked quietly. "I mean I read that file, and I thought I had the correct information before my eyes – for which, by the way, I'm going to kill my partner when he comes back from his honeymoon," he groused out. "He should have done his homework and not accept such a case. I mean, we're lawyers and, sometimes, we do defend people who don't deserve it, but not in such situations, like yours," he said furiously, clenching and unclenching his fists.

He took a few seconds to calm down, and then continued, pointing to her, "Then, there you were. I got to know you, and nothing I saw matched the image I already had in my head. Wouldn't you question your instincts, Nora?" Matt inquired softly.

'Especially when you've already been burnt,' he added in his mind caustically, always his steady gaze trained on her.

"Maybe, yes," she admitted with a noncommittal shrug.

She understood in a way, although she wasn't very comfortable with him knowing so much about her when she knew almost next to nothing about him.

"You know, we're not equal in anything," she pointed out.

"What the… heck, do you mean?" he groused, finding himself again in the situation of changing what he said in mid-sentence.

His language had worsened during the last few days and he knew where to place the blame.

"Well, let's see," she tapped a finger to her lips, suddenly feeling mean.

The day had strained her and it wasn't over yet. She needed to release some of the pant-up pressure, and she chose him to be the recipient. She knew she wasn't fair, but, that very moment, being fair seemed overrated.

"You seem to know everything about me, while I know next to nothing about you," she pointed out.

"You know plenty," he said, pushing away from the window.

With heavy steps, he came toward her.

"Come on, Nora! We've spent together a good part of a few days already. You must already have some knowledge about me. I know there are other things you need to find out and you will," he said.

Matt inhaled deeply to calm sudden doubts. Few people would accept his loony bin family, and especially their special skills.

"There might be things you'll dislike or which will make you run for safety, I know, but I won't hide anything from you," he stated with determination.

Now he loomed over her, not very comfortable with his decision of being completely open with her. That was something he'd never tried before. He'd always kept something secret, even from his parents and siblings.

"You have money, I have only a paycheck," she pointed out. "Even my savings have been lost when I contributed to the advance for the house," she explained in a disheartened voice.

"Yes, I know. It was the money you should have received after the divorce, and I made it impossible, I know," Matt nodded, in a bleak mood now, his nervous fingers running through his hair.

"Don't gloss over what I'm saying here, Matt," Nora snapped at him. "I didn't say I lost money because of you. I said you have money while I don't."

"Unimportant," he waved that argument away.

"How can you say it's unimportant? Rebecca already labelled me, and the remaining part of your family will soon follow suit," she said with exasperation.

"Some will," he admitted and sat next to her.

He took her hand in his again. Now, a smile played on his lips, and drove Nora crazy.

"How can you be so unconcerned about that?" she cried out. "Matt, I'm talking to you," she poked him, when she saw he was more concerned with her palm than what she was saying.

"I know you are," he looked up into her eyes, suddenly very serious. "I can guarantee there will be family members who will try to undermine your position and say vile things about you. It would have happened even if you'd had a fortune, or blue blood or whatever. Bryan went through all that, you know. If Becka and he survived, in the end, we will too, I promise you."

"I have a child," she reminded him.

"So? I can't see any problem there. The little imp is smart and sweet. And he is yours, so I have no issue with that."

"But others will," she replied quietly, and touched his face. "I might not be the best choice for you, Matt, even for a brief affair."

"First, I don't need a brief affair, Nora," he replied dryly. "If I wanted an affair, I wouldn't be here. Second, I don't care about the best choice," he said, watching her intensely. "I care about my choice."

He leaned and kissed her lips briefly and then stood up to walk his frustration.

"All right, we might have a fall out, today, tomorrow or next year. Or we might end up together," Matt said. Nettled, he turned back to her. "What will be, will be. We can't change it, Nora. But I'd be damned if I let some hypocrites dictate my actions and my choices," he boomed, and Nora's eyes opened wide.

"Very well said, son," a melodic voice came from the door.

CHAPTER THIRTEEN

Shocked, Nora and Matt turned like one. Someone had entered the room, and they hadn't noticed. A hushed cry flew off Nora's lips, but Matt's hand on hers, reassured her that everything was fine.

Marjorie Winston, and her husband Jonathan, stood just inside the door, holding hands, as always. Pride for her first born had brought tears in Marjorie's eyes.

Jonathan smiled at the younger couple with delight. Once, in the past, he'd been in the exact sore spot where his son stood now, and he understood better than anyone what Matt felt.

"Mother," Matt exclaimed with exasperation. "I thought we arranged to see each other when Nora was discharged," he reproached to her.

"I know, I know," she waved her hand. "I also know you'd have found a way to keep me away, afraid I'd try to meddle in your business, like grandma," she admonished him, waving her finger under his nose. "You should know me better than that, my first born," she chided him. "Plus, I needed a reason not to talk to grandma. She came just when we were leaving. We apologized because we were in a rush, and left her there," she said, and then, pensively, she continued, "I hope she won't still be there on the door stoop when we get back home. She didn't take it well, I must say."

Nora glanced at Matt, and the blush spreading on his face and neck surprised her.

"Care to make the introductions, Matty?" his father asked, amused, and his smile reflected in his dark eyes.

Curious, Nora studied Matt's parents. Matt didn't take after only one of them. He had his mother's eyes and father's coloring.

His mother seemed very serious and his father easy-going. Matt's temper was a combination of the two.

Matt sighed and glanced at Nora. He shrugged, took her hand and brought her in front of his parents.

"This is Nora, my girlfriend," he introduced her. "Nora, this is my nosy sweet mother, Marjorie Winston, and this is my father, who, if I know him well, and I do, has definitely been dragged here. He's Jonathan Winston."

Nora barely kept her laughter, however his father chuckled and slapped his son over the shoulder.

Marjorie scowled at Matt, and then took Nora's stretched hand. Yet, instead of shaking it, she pulled the younger woman into a hug.

Now, that astounded Nora. She'd expected a different welcome from Matt's parents. They certainly must have had higher expectations for their son, not a single, almost broke, mother.

She didn't even know what her financial situation was right then. Matt had helped her to fill in the forms for a disability claim two days before, but she still had to wait for an answer.

She awkwardly hugged Marjorie back, and no sooner had Marjorie released her, that Jonathan enveloped her in a bear-hug. As tall and well-built as Matt, Jonathan didn't bother to control his strength, and she yelped at the sudden pain.

Immediately, Matt pulled her in his arms, and, with a ferocious scowl, bellowed to his father, "She's hurt, damn it."

Then, he led her to the bed as if she'd come unglued before them, and nudged her to lie down.

"I don't want to lie down in front of your parents, Matt," she hissed. "I'm fine, it was just a twinge, really," she attempted to convince him, but he didn't have any of that.

"Who are you kidding now? If I didn't know the extent of your wounds…" Matt shook his head.

"I'm very sorry, Nora," Jonathan came and caressed her arm. "I haven't realized you were hurt," he explained.

"Why would she be in hospital if she weren't?" Matt growled, and everyone looked at him, as if he'd lost his mind.

"It's not like I knew the circumstances of her hospitalization," he reproached to his son.

"Don't worry about," Nora waved Jonathan's sincere concern away. Then, she turned to Matt, and, in a soft voice, she said, "It was just a twinge, really. I'm fine. I'll even talk to the doctor to discharge me in the morning," she explained, stroking his arm to soothe him.

"Allow him to worry, pumpkin," Marjorie told her.

She came to the bed as well and wedged in between the two men. Gently, but with steel determination, she helped Nora lie down, which made Matt very happy.

"You have to give a man his due, now and then. Their pride is a fragile thing, I'm afraid, and you need to placate them," she said, brushing Nora's hair away from her forehead.

"Hey!" an entire chorus of male protests came from around the room.

Nora peeked past Marjorie, and chuckled. Both Matt and Jonathan were scowling. Then she noticed the scowl of a third man, who'd come with Becka and Nat. It was a darn convention gathering in her room.

Unruffled, Marjorie patted her hand and turned to the others. She said with nonchalance, "It's true, you know."

Then she noticed the new people in the room, and greeted them, "Hi, Becka and Jay. I haven't seen you there."

"We've come just in time to hear you, auntie" Becka grinned. "And I absolutely agree with you," she nodded vigorously.

"Not you too," Jay complained.

"Who do we have here?" Marjorie looked at the toddler, who was clinging on to Becka's hand.

Nat hid behind Becka shyly, and Nora tried to jump off bed, only to be stopped by Matt.

"Easy, honey. My mom won't have him for dessert," he attempted to joke, but her glare told him he wasn't funny.

Then, he eased her up, in a sitting position.

"Stay here," he ordered, and she frowned.

Matt didn't pay attention to her frown, but called Nat to him. The boy came from behind Becka and launched himself at him, hugging his legs.

"Easy, Nat," Matt said, in the same voice he'd used with Nora. "Look, these are my parents," he turned the boy around, and pointed to Marjorie and Jonathan.

That was all it took for the boy. He forgot his shyness and greeted Matt's parents with a smile.

Marjorie showered him with compliments and made him feel important, and Jonathan shook his hand. Nat beamed with pride.

After a few minutes of inane chatter, Marjorie turned to Nora, "So, tomorrow, you want to be discharged. You know you can't go at home alone, especially with Nat. I doubt you could manage by yourself."

"I will, don't worry," Nora dismissed Marjorie's concerns.

She didn't want Marjorie to believe she'd be a burden, and she'd be clutching at her son.

Matt didn't even bother to tell her she was wrong. He just rode rough-shod over her words.

"Of course, she won't be alone. She and Nat will stay with me until she recovers. I understand it might take a few months."

"Matthew Winston," Nora glowered at him and pushed him, so she could stand. "I won't have you tell me what to do," she poked him in his chest with her finger.

"She has the same bad habit, mother, like you. She likes to poke," Matt chuckled.

Jonathan and Jay joined in his hilarity, which didn't endear them with the two women.

"Yep, that she does," Jay said and came next to Matt and elbowed him, a grin on his face.

However, neither Nora or Marjorie were amused with them. Nora raised a brow and stared Matt down, while Marjorie just gave them the evil eye.

Becka thought she'd better save what was left of that visit. The men seemed unaware of the bad currents, and the other two women were seething.

"I think Nora's correct if she wants to decide her own recovery, Matt," she said, and Matt glinted his eyes at her. "And I'm very sure she'll decide to live with you, and take advantage of your help with Nat. After all, we all know she loves Nat above all."

Nora knew she'd been trapped by Becka's words. She couldn't stubbornly insist she'd live by herself. She knew she had physical limitations for the moment, and didn't want to endanger her son. Yet, it didn't seem right to just move in with Matt.

Nat kept looking from an adult to another. He was confused because of their behavior, but he understood just fine that Matt wanted them to live with him.

"We'll go home with Matt, mommy, right?" he asked Nora, putting her on the spot again.

She sighed deeply and said, "We'll see, sweetie. Mommy will have to think it over, all right?"

CHAPTER FOURTEEN

Nora sat on the cushy pillow laid on the wide window sill, watching the marina. Matt's apartment had a superb view of the harbor and Nora had already learned to enjoy it.

The morning after meeting Matt's parents, Nora persuaded the doctor to discharge her. She promised she'd take it easy and start physiotherapy after two weeks.

Matt supported her and assured the doctor he'd make sure she'd not overtax her body. Of course, he took her to his apartment directly, and started doing just what he'd promised.

During that afternoon with Matt's parents, for Nat's sake, she'd accepted to go home with Matt, although she wasn't sure it was a smart move.

Whenever she thought of the encounter with Marjorie and Jonathan, she shook her head with dismay. That had been one of the most confusing afternoons she'd ever lived, and she wasn't sure she'd entirely understood what had happened.

Nora feared everything would crumble to her feet in no time. She'd had her doubts when Matt came to take her from the hospital the morning she was released. Some of those doubts didn't disappear during the following two days, although Matt had been very considerate, in his own way, ever since.

Matt offered her the third bedroom available in his apartment. That brought some relief. She'd feared he'd nurtured certain expectations, and she didn't think she could live up to them, not so early in their relationship anyway.

Her ex might have painted her in harlot's colors, but at heart, she was an old-fashioned woman. Aside from her ex-husband, she'd been involved with only one other man before her marriage. That relationship had lasted for almost three years.

She wasn't completely at ease in Matt's house, though, in spite of Matt's efforts to make her feel welcome. Not used to be underfoot and waited hand and foot, she worried that, one day, he might feel crowded or view her or her son as an imposition.

Living in the same house with him gave her more insight into the kind of man he was. She found out new things about him all the time, and she liked more and more the man she discovered.

Yet, one thing distressed her: Matt was overbearing. He didn't allow her to do anything, not even to carry her cup to the sink or dishwasher. He'd jump to his feet at once and nudge her to sit or lie down.

He expected her to obey his edict of not lifting a finger and rest as much as possible. If she didn't, discussions aroused.

Even when it came to Nat, they had arguments. She couldn't complain he tried to separate them. He was all for her to spend as much time as possible with her son, but only if she didn't try to take care of the boy's bath, for example, or prepare his food.

Bryan still supplied them with meals, and that embarrassed her to no end. Yes, she had a hard time standing and walking, but she could do most of the cooking sitting, in her opinion. Of course, Matt was deaf to any argument.

The thought he was so domineering drove her crazy. As result, they butted heads all the time, and they hadn't spent seventy-two hours together yet.

Every time a discussion aroused, Matt would lecture. He'd speak in a calm voice, as if he'd tried to pacify her. That tone of voice riled her more than if he'd shouted at her.

She had eyes and could see the twitch in his jaw or the flash of his eyes when she turned to be very stubborn. Yet, he pretended he wasn't upset, and left the impression she'd overreacted, as if he'd had to calm a child's tantrum.

The buzz of the intercom interrupted her ruminations. She glanced at the door surprised. Matt had left with Nat for ice-cream half an hour ago, but Nora doubted he didn't have the key.

For a moment, she thought to ignore the intercom, yet the person calling was stubborn enough and kept punching the code in. With her heart in her boots, Nora tiptoed to the door.

The intercom went finally silent, and she sighed satisfied with the respite. She turned to go back to her favorite spot, when the beeps began again and she jumped up. The sudden move jarred her leg, and she hissed at the piercing pain, tears welling in her eyes.

Now, her temper flushed, she pushed the key and asked in a belligerent voice, "Who's there?"

"Finally," Marjorie's melodious voice came and Nora froze. "We were concerned something happened to you. I've just spoken to Matt and he said you were alone at home," Marjorie said, and then, sighed with relief. "Buzz us in, Nora, dear," she asked.

Nora closed her eyes in defeat. She didn't even want to know who that '*us*' was. Far too many people were around Matt all the time. During the last few years, she'd learned to content herself with Nat's company. She didn't have family or a string of friends to visit her.

She pressed the button to open the door downstairs, and unlocked the apartment door. Then, she leaned on the wall, waiting for the group to come upstairs.

A few minutes later, a knock sounded on the door and she opened it. Stunned, she looked at the people crowded on the landing. She knew most of them. At least she's already met most of them.

Marjorie and Becka beamed at her and came in, leading the way for the others. Marjorie took one of her arms, and Becka the other. They both helped her to get to the sofa without allowing her to put much weight on the injured leg.

The others followed, chatting with each other, and carrying bags in their hands.

Nora couldn't understand that family. They baffled her. Ironically, she understood Rebecca. Her behavior was predictable. Theirs wasn't. She couldn't believe they'd visit with her and not berate her for laying her hands on their golden boy, Matt, as Rebecca said.

Marjorie sat next to Nora with a whimsical smile on her face, and patted her hand, as if she'd known what thoughts crossed the woman's mind.

"This is my husband, Bryan," Becka motioned a tall, well-built man to come and make Nora's acquaintance.

Nora's eyes swept over the strong shoulders and prominent cheekbones. She noted the scar on his left cheek, but didn't react. She beamed at him, grateful for everything he'd done for her son and herself.

"Nice to meet you," he said, shaking her hand. "I'm going to put the food in the fridge," he winked at her. "You'll have enough for about three days, now. Some of it will go into the freezer, but Matt is capable enough to microwave it," he grinned.

"Jonathan, take our bags to the kitchen, as well," Marjorie asked her husband, in the voice of a general.

He just saluted her jokingly. First, he came to Nora, kissed her cheek and asked, "Is everything fine? Does my boy treat you right?"

Taken aback, Nora couldn't formulate an answer and just nodded.

"Good, then," Jonathan approved, patted her shoulder, and sauntered in the direction of the kitchen.

"Have you cooked as well?" Nora asked Marjorie with dismay.

"Of course, dear. I mean I knew Bryan cooked for you, but I had to contribute with something," Marjorie explained with a shrug. "What kind of mother would I be if I let others take care of my children, huh?"

Nora didn't know how to answer and wide-eyed, she just stared at her. For a moment, she thought Marjorie had taken a pot-shot at her because she did let someone else take care of her son. Marjorie rubbed her arm, and beamed at her some more, until Nora thought she'd simply scream.

"Now, let's see... You know Jay already," Marjorie continued, as if she hadn't noticed Nora's confusion and distress.

Jay waved at her, and the grin on his lips told Nora he knew what she was thinking. She wondered what he'd say if she wiped that grin off his lips with a well-aimed fist. Those Winstons played with her mind.

"This is our daughter, Maggie. She's Jay's twin," she specified, the ghost of a smile in the corner of her mouth.

Nora understood why. Maggie and Jay looked anything but alike. Jay had inherited his father's eyes, and his hair was dark blond, while Maggie had her mother's eyes and her father's coloring, like Matt. Anyone would have guessed Maggie and Matt were siblings. Jay was more difficult to place in the family, if one didn't know his mother, as well.

"Hey, there," Maggie greeted her with exuberance, almost hopping in place, her curls going this way and that way.

At the tone of her voice, Nora winced inwardly. She just knew Matt's sister was one of those women with excess of energy, who were busy all the time and never stopped to rest or smell the roses. Nora wasn't a slacker herself, but people like Maggie exhausted her just with their presence.

Nora merely waved back with a shy smile, and Maggie, her dark hair bouncing in thick and silky curls, tucked her legs under her on the carpet, next to the armchair Jay had already claimed.

"This is Lily," Marjorie presented the other young woman in the room. "Lily is my niece, and Matt's cousin," she explained.

Lily shook Nora's hand with warmth, but she didn't have Maggie's enthusiasm. Nora's eyes took everything in - the tall and slender silhouette, the short curvy red hair and dark blue eyes. Lily was exactly what she wasn't, and she seemed of the same age or maybe a couple of years younger.

"I'll take the cakes and snacks out of the bags," Lily said, looking at Marjorie, and then she attacked the bag close to her.

The bags, with the exception of the bags Bryan and Jonathan carried into the kitchen, had been left next to the coffee table. Nora had imagined they'd been shopping. The thought they'd brought cakes and snacks for the visit didn't cross her mind.

"I should be the one offering you some coffee or cakes," she suddenly realized.

She tried to stand up and go search Matt's kitchen. It wasn't her house, true enough, but she lived there for the time being and she had to play the hostess role.

"Don't be silly," Marjorie stopped her. "You may hold with ceremony when you have friends or acquaintances in the house, but we're family. Matt would never talk to me again if I'd let you go through all that trouble," she shook her head at Nora.

"You only have to get used to having a large family," Becka laughed.

"Not easy, believe me," her husband, who was just coming back from the kitchen, carrying two platters with hors-d'oeuvre, replied. "By the way," he said to everybody, "Jonathan is making coffee. I boiled some water to make some tea for you, Becka," he told his wife, who thanked him with a nod.

"But you're the guests in the house… I mean… I…," Nora started stuttering.

The idea that they might think she was actually the guest in that house swiftly dawned on her. She couldn't contradict them - they were right.

"We are the guests, that's true," Maggie said, "but you are in convalescence, and that gives us the right to change roles," she waved her worries aside.

"I didn't mean…" Nora tried to explain, but Jonathan, coming with coffee and cups, interrupted her.

"But you should," he said putting everything on the table. "If I know my Matt, you have the right to think you're in your house and we're just guests."

"No, no, no, I didn't mean…"

"Don't trouble yourself," Marjory took her hand. "Matt will be here in no time and I don't want to explain to him why you're agitated and how we upset you."

"Matt's stubborn enough not to talk to us for a year," Jay remarked and Nora stared at him. Disbelief and shock marked her face, for everyone to see.

Matt and Nat chose that exact moment to arrive.

CHAPTER FIFTEEN

When Nat learned they had guests, he didn't want to linger in the ice-cream shop anymore. He insisted on going back home at once.

Matt didn't argue with him. He needed to be there as well, and shield Nora from any possible attacks, so they rushed back home.

Now, Matt glanced at Nora and saw the shock on her face. He'd already worried, but now he became livid, and his ire narrowed his eyes and his nostrils flared.

He asked in a stern voice, "Now, who upset Nora and how? What did you say to her?"

Much to his dismay, their reactions to his words weren't what he'd expected. He'd expected excuses or explanations, but none came.

Jay and Maggie burst into laughter and howled like hyenas. Nora tried to say something, opened her mouth, but nothing came out. His mother glared at him and shook her head in disapproval.

"Now, Matt, is this a way to talk to your parents?" she chastised him.

"If you distressed her…" Matt started saying, but his father came to him and slapped him on the shoulder.

"Call back the troops, son," he said with a chuckle. "Nobody declared any kind of war here. Nora simply can't believe we take care of our people and we consider her part of the family now. No need to blow a fuse over that," he shook his head to his first born.

Matt looked around and felt ashamed. He picked a thought here and there and realized his father was telling the truth.

He'd assumed a lot of wrong things. No one was guilty of anything and were openly making fun of him.

"Come on, brother," Maggie said from her spot near Jay, "lighten up. We're not here to upset Nora, but the opposite. And we brought gifts, by the way," she mentioned and pointed to the snacks Lily was still setting on the table.

Lily knew Matt and took his outburst in stride. Matt always jumped to defend people who couldn't defend themselves. She imagined he'd seen Nora as the sacrificial lamb when he found her in the middle of his close-knit family.

"So you're all right," he said to Nora, although he didn't sound very confident.

Nora just nodded and stretched her hand to Nat who came to her immediately.

"We bought ice-cream for you too, mommy. Matt asked what you liked best and bought you pistachio," he said, although his tongue knotted around the word *'pistachio'*.

Everyone smiled and Nora kissed the top of his head, "That's awesome, baby. I can't wait to taste it."

"Not before you try my pastries, I hope," Marjorie intervened.

"You're in for a treat," Lily said, finally finishing fussing with the food. "Aunt Marjorie is the best when it comes to baking."

"I wouldn't sell Bryan so short," Becka contradicted her, a scowl on her face. "His pastries are heavenly, so that you know."

"Thank you, sweetheart," Bryan said with a self-deprecating laugh. "That's what a man wants to be praised for -- his pastries."

"Come on, Bryan, everyone knows how macho you are," she blew off his concerns.

"That's true," Jay noted. "You have nothing to worry about. One look at you, and no one would give a thought to your pastries, Bryan."

"What do you mean?" Becka asked in an icy voice, measuring him.

"Becka, Becka, Becka," Jay shook his head. "The man rivals a mountain. One look coming from those steely eyes of his, and no one would dare to say anything to him."

"But Rebecca," Bryan corrected him, and another round of laughter burst out.

"Oh, man, I won't ever forget what happened when she met you that first time," Jonathan slapped his knee. "Matt, you need more seats around here. How come I haven't noticed that before?" he wondered.

"Because you've never come in groups," Matt observed dryly. "I'll make sure to add more furniture in the near future. Now, let's borrow the chairs from the breakfast table and…" he frowned, thinking what else to bring in.

He thought of the bar stools in the kitchen, but they weren't very cozy for a chat in the living-room. He also had a chair in his den, but nothing else.

"I'm okay," Bryan said.

He left the tea he'd brought for Becka on the coffee table, and then, pulled Becka up. After he took her seat, he lowered her in his lap.

"Nat will seat in my lap," Marjorie demanded.

She waved to the boy, calling him to her, which he did immediately -- another surprise for Nora.

"I'm good," Maggie told Matt from where she sat on the carpet.

He knew she was. Maggie rarely sat in an armchair or on a sofa, if she could sit on the floor with her legs tucked under her. Many made fun of her, calling her the gypsy of the family.

"So, you need only two chairs," Lily made the math for him. "One for me and one for you," she waved her hand around to the others who were all seated.

"Right, two chairs coming up," Matt attempted to joke.

He wanted to lighten the mood because he felt awkward after accusing his family of nefarious endeavours. Then, he brought the chairs from the breakfast table.

***

Nora lay down on her bed, sated with food and laughter and fun. She'd felt out of her element when Matt's family came to visit, but that changed once everyone was pushing food on to her and recounted stories of a much younger Matty.

She'd felt included. She was the centre of attention, although sometimes, either Matt or his mother fanned too much over her.

A couple of times, she even rolled her eyes, which amazed her. She hadn't done that since her high-school years.

Some of the stories they told had been either very touching or very rambunctious, but she enjoyed them all. She also enjoyed seeing Matt blush a few times.

He couldn't touch her because he was seated across from her, yet, she was aware of his intense gaze all the time. She even felt the caress of his dark-blue pupils all over her skin, whenever his eyes swept over her.

Sometimes, her heart would trot faster and she wondered how Marjorie didn't hear it. At the same time, she got hotter and hotter under that intensity and the waves of desire coming from him. Those raw sensations, which she didn't want or afford to feel right then, bothered her a lot.

Despite Matt's opposition, Marjorie and Jonathan shared their memories about Matt as a toddler. Sometimes, she laughed hearing about his antics, but mostly, her feelings for Matt grew a little more.

His siblings and cousins told stories about him as a teenager. They were so good in recounting those times, she could almost see Matt, as a teenager, always chased by girls or ready to play an inoffensive prank, which would land him up in the principal's office.

Maggie's stories were the most outrageous. Some of the things she related shocked her parents. Apparently, they were completely unaware such things had happened in their children's life during their adolescence. Jonathan laughed heartily, but Marjorie had to fan herself a few times.

Once, Matt growled and threatened his sister, promising serious payback if she didn't stop. Maggie just laughed at him, and high-fived Jay, who supported and contributed to all her stories.

For Nora, it had been a magical afternoon and evening. She'd never experienced so much camaraderie between family members. Her family had never shared such joyful and touching moments.

Yet, something bothered her. Sometimes someone would begin to tell a story, and, suddenly, all eyes turned to them in warning. Immediately, they'd changed their story in mid-sentence. She even surprised a few imperceptible shakes of the head. Every time, Bryan mused, and an ironic smile appeared on his lips, as if he'd been in on the secret.

She was sure they hid something from her. She didn't know what, but intended to find out. She felt as if it were something very important and decisive for the evolution of her relationship with Matt.

Light knocks on the door drew her back to the present. She hesitated a fleeting second, but then she softly said, "Come in."

Matt opened the door and stopped. He'd mussed his hair again, undoubtedly by running his fingers through it. She'd noticed that habit several times and found it charming.

Dressed only in dark slacks and a white shirt, which defined his shoulders and was open half way down, he looked good to eat. Too bad she was on a strict diet.

He looked her over, his dark-blue eyes getting darker while sweeping over her sleeveless nightie. The cotton hugged the curves of her body in the right places, and, unaware, he licked his lips.

He looked his fill and then, said, "I saw you still had the light on… I imagined you were still awake so… I thought we could… talk, maybe. I don't feel like going to bed already," he explained with some difficulty.

Matt massaged the base of his nose. It wasn't like him not to find his words, but his world had changed dramatically lately, and he felt like walking in a haze.

"Yes, of course," she said.

She sat up carefully. Her movements didn't pain her so much now when most of the soreness was gone.

She leaned back on the headboard. His eyes followed the fall of the thick red mass of hair over her shoulders.

With a pat on the bed, she invited him to sit. He hurried to do so, after closing the door. It was more than he'd expected when he decided to come to her room.

"I hear if Nat wakes up, don't worry," he thought to assure her. "Are you very tired?" he asked, concern showing in his eyes. "I know a lot of people visited tonight and you're still in convalescence. I saw it on your face, you know. The exhaustion, I mean. It was obvious you were tired."

"Oh, that's why you rushed everybody out," she guessed, and he nodded.

"You shouldn't have," she said, shaking her head. "Yes, I felt a little tired now and then, but that's because I'm not used to such gatherings, Matt," she stroked his strong forearm with a featherlike touch, and a shiver ripped through his body. She thought she'd imagined everything and continued, "But everybody had fun, including me."

"I'm glad you enjoyed their company, Nora. I love the others in the family, even Rebecca sometimes, but the people who were here tonight are the ones I love the most. If you feel good in their company, then it's perfect," he said, half-facing her, playing with her fingers and looking intently into her eyes.

He'd touched her fingers several times by then. The first time, his touch had surprised her.

She'd have thought the skin on a lawyer's fingers and palms was smooth, yet Matt's wasn't. His skin was rough and, every time he slid his fingers over hers, she felt the touch deep in her core.

"You do some physical labor, don't you?" she asked before she was even aware she'd opened her mouth.

She cringed when the meaning of her own words dawned on her. He chuckled when she closed her eyes with dismay.

"You know you can ask me anything," he said softly, his fingers touching her wrist and sliding up on her forearm.

She shook her head and licked her bottom lip. Then, she opened her eyes and said, "You're touching my hands and arms all the time."

"I'd love to touch all of you all the time," he admitted, and her eyes rounded. "Don't worry, Nora, I know you need time, and not only to recover physically. I know you're not ready to open yourself to me emotionally now," Matt said very matter-of-factly, and touched the side of her face. "But a man still can hope," he chuckled with self-deprecation.

"What if I'm never ready?" she inquired in a whispered voice.

He shrugged and bowed his head, his eyes following the finger he slid up and down on the inside of her arm. Then, he looked up at her, a strange light in his eyes.

"I'm a grown-up, I'll survive," he shrugged again. "It wouldn't be like I could blame you or force you to like or love me," he pointed out.

"I like you just fine, Matt," she said, and brushed the hair off his forehead.

Matt, always watching her intently, leaned over her and touched his mouth to hers. She sighed and cradled his face in her hands, opening her lips for him.

Matt braced on one arm on the bed and then, kissed her softly, his lips learning hers. His kiss was hesitant at first, but became more confident.

He didn't hurry and kept his kiss sweet, taking his time to savor her taste. He didn't want to arouse her, but to help her recognize his body as her mate. Yet, he could feel her tremble next to him, and his male ego felt satisfied.

His fingers slid over her right arm, in a hypnotic rhythm, leaving goosebumps on her skin in their wake. He changed the angle of his kiss and his fingers reached to her waist, resting on the roundness of her hip for a few seconds.

"Would you lie down to be more comfortable?" he asked, his lips almost touching hers.

The heat inside her spiked when she felt the words forming over her lips. She shimmied down, almost without thinking.

Her fingers burrowed into his forearms for support. Her nightie hiked up on her thighs, and Matt breathed deeply when his eyes swept over her legs.

Braced on his elbow, he stretched next to her, his head in his palm. His other hand lazily stroked the side of her face, and then cupped her chin.

He leaned down and when his mouth was a hair's breadth away from hers, he whispered, "I'd love to kiss you some more, Nora. But only if you're comfortable with that."

He searched her glimmering eyes, but they didn't reveal anything. Then, he tried to read her mind, and see for himself what she thought, and as always, came out blank.

"Yes, please," she replied softly, and he felt her breath on his lips.

Now, he needed to kiss her, more than anything. His hand slid from her chin and caressed the side of her neck.

His lips settled on hers, and he sighed. She swallowed the sound and answered with a sigh of hers, and he felt a jolt of awareness in his lower body.

While his lips molded hers, his fingers stroked her shoulder and arm, down to her wrist. His fingers intertwined with hers, while his kiss became more daring and deeper.

He stopped only when both of them needed to come up for air. They breathed hard, and Nora's lips were rosy and slightly puffy. His fingers were still closed on hers, and his thumb stroked the inside of her wrist.

Matt's eyes were locked on Nora's face. She still had her eyes closed, but then, when her respiration quieted, she opened them slowly. The heat in her pupils kicked Matt squarely in his chest.

"I'd love to touch you everywhere, Nora, but I don't dare. I think I'll try not to think of that for at least another week, baby," he confessed.

Nora didn't do anything more than look at him. After a few seconds, she blinked and licked her lips.

"You know you're killing me here, honey," Matt said with a chuckle, yet his voice wasn't as confident as usual. "You never say anything and I don't know what you think."

"Oh, I think plenty, Matt," she replied in a dry voice. "The problem's everything is confusing. I know I want you and I can see you want me, but I don't know if it is all right, or it is too soon or if you want just that," she shrugged.

"Wow, all that," Matt laughed. "You know you don't have to make up your mind right this moment. About anything," he assured her, smoothing her hair.

Then, he took a thick lock between his fingers. He lifted to his face, and brushed it to his cheek.

"No, I can't make up my mind now," she replied ruefully. "I need time, probably more than a week," she warned him.

"Sweetheart, you can take a month or two, or as long as you need," he said and kissed her forehead.

They lay in silence for a few minutes, Matt always braced on the elbow, and his other hand stroking her arm, her hip, and, in a very daring moment, her thigh. Nora kept watching his face. The emotions playing on his face and in his eyes captivated her.

"You want something from me," she suddenly said, and his eyes came fast back to hers.

"How do you know?" he frowned.

"I can see it on your face," she replied. "It's hard to miss it."

"I see," he said. "I thought you've read my mind," he replied mildly.

She giggled at his words, and that surprised him. He'd never heard her giggle and didn't think she'd be the woman to do that.

"Come on, Matt, I'm a grown woman. I don't believe in fairy-tales and paranormal things. I do believe there's an explanation for everything," she stressed out. "Like now," she said. "I knew you wanted something because I could see it in your eyes. No one's capable to read minds," she shook her head with determination.

"If you say so," Matt accepted her explanation, although he felt a sort of hurt. Yet, he couldn't come out and say, *Hey, I can read your mind*. Quite inaccurate. He couldn't read her mind.

"So, what do you want?" she asked again.

"I don't know what you'd think," he started hesitantly, "but I was thinking..." he said and stopped.

"Come on, Matt, don't be shy. You've been anything but shy until now," she laughed.

"I was wondering if you'd like to sleep with me," he snapped, uncomfortable with what he had to say and annoyed with her amusement.

"Smooth," she said gingerly, and touched her upper lip with her tongue.

"I'm not talking about... I'm talking about sleeping, you know, that activity people do at night, to regenerate or whatever," he clarified his idea, miffed by her comment.

"Oh, I see," she smiled. "Really? Just sleeping? Why would you want that?" she suddenly frowned.

"Because I want to feel you next to me," he admitted. "And because we might feel more emotionally comfortable afterward, or... I don't really know why," he admitted. "But I know I do."

"So, to be clear," she said, turning on one side to face Matt, and held her head with her hand, copying his posture. "You want to sleep next to me, to hold me in your arms, and nothing more," she said, and her voice showed her bafflement.

"Yes, that's what I want. I told you I wouldn't touch you otherwise, even if you wanted it. You wouldn't enjoy anything right now, anyway, considering your wounds."

"Probably not," Nora conceded. "Do I have a minute or two to think?" she asked him, in a playful tone.

"Take as long as you need," he murmured, and his hand rested on her hip.

Nora closed her eyes and touched his chest with her palm. He knew she was pondering the pros and cons because a serious frown formed between her eyebrows. He wanted to reach out and smoothen the frown away, but resisted the impulse. He knew it wouldn't have been fair to touch her and muddle her mind, but for a moment there, he didn't care about what was fair.

Her fingers drummed on his chest and each touch drove him mad. Blood pulsated in his temples, and his arousal increased tenfold. He clenched his teeth, and thanked God her eyes were closed.

After something that felt like hours, she opened her eyes, smiled at him, and said, "All right. Nothing wrong if we share a bed and body heat," she explained her decision.

"Romantic," he noticed dryly. "I don't know about the body heat," he continued. "It's summer already, if you haven't noticed."

"Yes, I noticed, Matt," she snickered and patted his chest. "I was just joking. I hope you know that," she suddenly looked up, straight into his eyes, and he saw genuine concern.

"Yes, I know," he grinned at her.

"And how do we do that?" she asked.

"I thought you'd never ask," he joked. "Let's take my bed," he proposed. "I had it order-made and I am comfortable in it. This one here is only a regular king."

"You mean to say you've offered me the low-quality bed?" she pretended to be affronted.

Matt laughed and flicked her nose.

"You're a laugh a minute, you know that," he replied. "No, smarty-pants, your bed isn't low-quality, but you're tiny and it's big enough for you. Anyway, you'll share my bed now, so you can't complain anymore," he said and in a fluid move, he stood up and took her hand. "Come on, let's see how you like my giant bed," he grinned at her and helped her stand.

Then, Matt knelt and finding her slippers, slid them on her feet. She giggled again. Although he'd abhorred giggles before, he liked how she sounded. Now though, he put a finger on her lips, "Shush, you'll wake Nathan."

Nora pretended to zip her lips and he chuckled. Their fingers intertwined, and he pulled her after him. They moseyed to his bedroom, Matt always taking care to match her slow gait.

When he opened the door, she stopped and looked around in awe.

"My God, this is much more than a bedroom," she whispered.

His bed was wide enough for at least four people to sleep without touching each other. The thick carpet, in warm autumn colors, stretched from wall to wall, and two armchairs and a small table nestled inside an alcove in one corner of the room.

"I gather you like it," he said dryly.

"You could say that," she nodded with enthusiasm. "Much better, more colorful and with more personality than the other one," she added, and grinned at him.

"Now, you share it, as well," he shrugged. "The ensuite bathroom is that way," he showed her a door on the right. "Tomorrow morning, I'll bring your things from the other bath so you could use this one. After Nat, of course," he grinned. "He always uses my bath in the morning, sorry."

"Yeah, I noticed," she said. "I expected him to come to me in the mornings, and to be honest, I felt somewhat betrayed when I noticed he came to you instead," she replied.

"Better me than you," he remarked and her eyes widened.

"What do you mean?" she glared.

"I imagine he likes to jump on you in the morning. I haven't had a morning without him bouncing up and down on me. With your wounds, that wouldn't be what your doctor recommended," he pointed out, an eyebrow hiking up his forehead.

"Oh, I forgot about that habit," she laughed briefly, and then grimaced. "How could I forget?"

"You've had enough to deal with. Let's hope he continues to choose my body for his morning amusement," Matt said and stroked the side of her face with the back of his hand. "Now, are you ready to turn in?" he asked her.

Nora nodded hesitantly, and then, shyly, she headed to the bed.

"What side do you prefer?" she asked without turning to him.

"Any of them is good for me," he replied.

Matt helped her climb onto the bed, and then, after she lay down, he covered her with the bed linen.

Matt turned off the light and crept into bed next to her. He slid his arm around her and, gently, pulled her to him. Once they settled, he opened his fingers on her abdomen and a satisfied sigh sounded in Nora's ear.

Nora felt her skin burning under his fingers, and long-forgotten sensations ran through her body.

It felt good in Matt's arms. His body almost surrounded her completely and, to her surprise, she discovered a sense of security and protection in his arms, which she'd never felt before.

"If you need to sleep more tomorrow, you can," he whispered, his lips nearly touching her ear, and she shivered. Matt pulled her closer, thinking she was cold.

"Becka said you'd promised we'd go sailing tomorrow," she whispered back, and her hand rested on top of his on her belly.

"I know, baby, but that will be at eleven. We won't stay long on the lake tomorrow," he promised her. "Just a couple of hours. We'll spend more time when we go to that get-together to Bryan's house on the island, okay? I don't want you to overdo it right now," Matt explain and his concern touched her.

"That's fine with me," she replied, and caressed his fingers.

"Good," Matt said. "Now, sleep baby," he asked her, and his lips touched her face.

CHAPTER SIXTEEN

That was Nora's fourth outing on Matt's yacht and she'd started to wait for those trips with impatience. Nora loved the feel of the wind in her hair and the smell of the water. Everything was different there – the light and sounds, the air and silence.

She couldn't wait to see Bryan's house on the lake, which Becka had praised so much. She was as giddy as Nat whenever she thought of that Saturday.

Maggie and Lily had taken an exuberant Nat to the bow. They chatted and laughed together. The boy kept asking questions, barely giving them the time to answer any of them, and that amused the women to no end.

Nora smiled. Those days, Nat could ask questions faster than anyone could answer. More than that, the lake fascinated him and he was curious about everything. He'd already expressed the wish of becoming a sailor one day. She was just thankful that day was far away.

Before the shooting, Nora had taken him on a stroll on the shore now and then, but she'd never had the time to linger. She'd always had too many things to do, and she didn't have the luxury of longer strolls or outings. She always felt guilty because she couldn't offer Nat such luxuries, but she'd promised herself she would one day.

Now, with the lake always in sight from Matt's windows, her son had become crazy about it. She couldn't deny she had also fallen in love with the lake.

Marjorie and Jonathan sat next to her on the benches shadowed by a huge colorful canopy. After they chatted her for over a quarter of an hour, now, they whispered between them and let her be.

Nora contented herself with watching the men man the yacht. Her mouth watered at the powerful display of muscles on their backs and arms.

Jay and Josh looked good enough, but they wouldn't hold a candle to Matt. He was taller and brawnier than the two other men. His dark coloring made him look very dashing, and she couldn't take her eyes away from him.

A seagull speared the sky and cried out, and startled her from her reverie. She shadowed her eyes and looked in the direction of Bryan's power yacht, which was also full of people.

His in-laws had joined them for the get-together. They were on the deck, fanning over the babies, and the corners of Nora's mouth lifted in a crooked smile. Nothing like a baby to make grown-up people sappy.

Nora had met Emilie and Gabriel a few days ago when they came by Matt's apartment for a brief visit. It was obvious they'd come to ogle her, and that had made her very self-conscious.

She should have got used to it by then. Lately, it had been a constant parade through Matt's house. One evening, Matt even observed dryly that his apartment had never seen so much traffic in years.

Beyond Bryan's yacht, the sail of his friend's yacht was visible. Bryan had invited Max to spend the day with them, not only because he needed another boat for all the people coming to his lake house. Max was his partner in the dojo and his best friend, and they got along very well.

Nora caught a glimpse of Ariel's straight blond hair, flying into the wind. She stood alone at the bow, looking into the distance.

Nora had noticed Ariel was slightly uncomfortable with Max, and she suspected Max was making Ariel jumpy and all too aware of her being a woman.

Alex and Max worked together, manning the yacht, and Michael and Amelie huddled on a bench on the deck.

Nora liked all of them, although Ariel and Alex had seemed somewhat cold and reserved toward her. She didn't know if they didn't like her or they were simply more reserved than the others. She shrugged – she didn't really care one way or the other.

She'd got to know Maggie and Jay better, and she'd made fast friends with Becka and Bryan. They were warm and friendly, so it wasn't hard to relate to them.

She'd already spent over two weeks in Matt's apartment. Although she felt better now, and she'd even started her physiotherapy, she found it hard to broach the subject of her leaving his house. She'd got used being around him, and the thought of not seeing him again made her sick.

Not that Matt seemed willing to give her an opening to discuss her imminent leaving. Whenever he asked about her health, he always changed the subject before getting to the point where she would claim she'd manage by herself and had to move back home. She didn't know how, because her disability pay covered only the rent, but she had to find a way.

Nora had spent all her nights in his bed. Matt would hold her, always careful not to give her any reason for discomfort. Yet, he always seemed to envelop her completely.

She didn't recall she'd ever had such a restful sleep in her entire life. Matt made her feel protected and cherished.

He never asked anything from her and never went beyond a few kisses -- all right, quite hot kisses. He truly intended not to rush things and demand anything from her, and his consideration baffled her. It was obvious he'd wanted more, but he never pressured her.

Nora turned around and brushed her hair off her face. She sighed deeply. She knew everything would change once she moved out of his house. That feeling of well-being and security would disappear. She also wondered if he'd still take the trouble to come around when she wasn't underfoot.

"Anything the matter, Nora?" Matt asked, sliding his arms around her from behind and brushing his lips on the side of her face.

"No, not really," she smiled, looking up at him and covering his hands with hers. "Just enjoying the surroundings."

"Yeah, sure," he replied in that dry voice she loved so much. "That's why you're sighing, right."

"No, really. I do enjoy being on the lake," she said, leaning her head back on his chest, her eyes always on his.

"That I know," he said.

He stared intently into her eyes first. His eyes always seemed to harbor mysteries and secrets she couldn't imagine. Then, he looked at her lips, and his fingers burrowed unconsciously in her midriff.

"How come you know?" she said lightly.

"It's on your face, baby," he answered pushing his chin forward. "It's not like I can read your mind," he mumbled, and she laughed.

"Good to know," she said. "You might run for cover if you read my mind," she teased him.

"I doubt that very much," he said and leaned over her to steal a kiss.

It was almost over before it started, but her lips still tingled and her fingers quivered on his hands.

"Later, baby," he whispered. "We're almost there," he explained, kissed her again and left.

Nora turned to see if they'd arrived at their destination, and her eyes fell on Marjorie and Jonathan, who were smiling at her with deep satisfaction. She'd completely forgotten about them, and now a blush spread all over her face.

Jonathan laughed heartily, and Marjorie, smacking him for his lack of subtlety, told Nora, "Don't mind us, Nora, dear. We just love to see you and Matt like that."

She patted Nora's leg and left it at that. She turned to her husband and began lecturing him in an undertone.

Nora couldn't understand Matt's parents. They should have been furious she'd insinuated herself into their son's life.

Matt was a renowned attorney and had amassed a fortune. She was just a paramedic, who, right then, was paid a little over half her salary, because of her health issues, and that would continue for at least half a year, as her doctor warned her.

Nora shook her head and gave up understanding their reasons. She went back to watching the men, busy with the approach maneuvers.

CHAPTER SEVENTEEN

The party had been going strong for several hours already. Nora wondered how they weren't exhausted yet. She'd sat on a blanket most of the time and felt a little tired.

They'd arrived at Bryan's house a little after ten and the food was arranged on a few folding tables. They spread blankets under the trees, in the shadow, and ate heartily, laughing, talking and teasing each other.

Nat had his nap inside Bryan's house. Marjorie and Jonathan, but also Michael and Amelie, and Gabriel and Emilie, rested in the house with the children, while the younger generation played volley.

Jay invited them to a card game, which made everyone throw something at him. They laughed while egging him, but Jay still seemed somewhat hurt.

Nora didn't understand why and no one offered to explain. Feeling bad for Jay, she told him she'd play with him, but Matt stopped her.

"You know I don't like to say you can't do something, baby, but, in this matter, I have to.

You'll never play cards with Jay," he said in a stern voice.

"But why?" she asked with exasperation, taking exception with his haughty manner. "Why everyone is reacting like this? Does he cheat?" she asked.

Jay groaned loudly, as if she'd just stabbed him in the back, and covered his face with his hands, bursting into laughter.

Matt smiled whimsically and shook his head.

"No, he doesn't cheat, but you still won't play with him. I know you're probably bored out of your mind, but if you want to play cards, you can play with me," he offered her, a crooked smile on his lips.

"I'm not bored," she replied through tight teeth. "You can go and play," she shooed him away.

"You won't get rid of me so easy, sweetie," Matt countered and lay down next to her on the blanket.

He noticed she was peeved, and he'd already spent too much time away from her. He'd been painfully aware of her, and kept her in his sight all the time, but he had to play with his siblings and cousins for a while. Otherwise, he'd never heard the end of it. They'd have mocked him he was besotted, which was the truth, of course, but he didn't feel like being the butt of their jokes.

Nora shrugged and turned her head to the group of young people resuming their fun. Ariel took off her shirt and shorts. Underneath she wore a black one-piece swimsuit, which hugged her body like a glove. Nora snickered when she noticed Max's eyes bulging out.

"What's so funny?" Matt asked and looked in the same direction.

He immediately saw Max's reaction and scowled.

"Ariel will make mincemeat out of him," he grumbled, unsure if he liked Max's attention for his cousin or not.

"Why?" Nora turned to him curious.

"Ariel is fastidious by far. She doesn't even like Bryan. She just tolerates him," Matt shrugged. "Imagine how she feels about this guy."

When he saw she didn't like how it sounded, he hurried to explain.

"Don't take me wrong, honey. I love Bryan. He's like a brother to me, you've seen it. And I have nothing against Max. I know him well. Hell, I've sparred with the man and we went out in a group a few times. I like him just fine. He's steady and honest. But Ariel... I don't see her going for his ponytail or his goatee," he shook his head. "And that might be her loss," Matt remarked. "Max might be the right man to mollify her a little. She's too stiff by half."

Nora leaned on him and he enveloped her in his arms.

"Maybe she'll try to know him better," she said quietly, watching Ariel heading for the shore to swim.

Matt observed Max taking off his shorts, and following her. Max's thoughts were loud enough, and Matt snickered.

"I think I'll put my money on him," he said, and his fingers burrowed underneath Nora's shirt.

Everybody had carped at her to take it off. It was a very warm and sunny day, and it must have been uncomfortable to wear it. Yet, self-conscious, afraid her scars would draw eyes, she'd refused.

Her abdomen quivered under his palm, and a smiled lifted the corner of his mouth. His mouth found the hollow between her neck and shoulder and kissed her.

"Matt," she panted for breath, and tried to still his hands. "We're in the open. Everyone can see us."

"So what?" he groused.

His lips trailed the column of her neck up, until they found the sensible spot he'd already discovered behind her ear.

"I don't care. They've guessed we're together by now, and if they haven't, then I've been wrong about their intellects all along," he whispered.

His tongue touched her earlobe and she shuddered. A faint moan reached his ears, and satisfied, he nibbled at her.

His fingers gently touched and massaged the skin on her abdomen and up until he reached underneath the soft curve of her breasts.

He didn't dare to continue his journey. He'd been continuously aroused for two weeks now, and he didn't think he could behave himself if he went into forbidden territory.

Matt breathed deeply and put his chin on the top of her head. He could do with holding her for the moment.

Not even five minutes later, Nat ran out of the house like a tornado, and came to them.

"I'm up, mommy. Hi, Matt. You said we swim when I wake up," he rushed to say.

Matt chuckled, kissed the top of Nora's head, and told her, "Sorry, honey, duty calls."

"You'll take care of him, Matt," she said, but her voice sounded inquiring.

"You can trust me. I won't let anything happen to him," he replied in a serious voice, and kissed her mouth briefly. "He'll also wear a safety vest, so don't worry."

"I should come too," she said nibbling at her bottom lip.

"And do what?" Matt asked irritated.

It wasn't as if she could jump into the lake and save Nat if anything had happened. However, seeing how irked she was, he changed his mind.

"All right, I'll spread the blanket right there on the shore, so you could keep an eye on us," he offered.

"I can spread the blanket myself," she retorted, but he didn't want to hear a thing.

He pulled her up, picked up the blanket and moseyed with her to the shore. Nat was hopping, happy to get into the water at last.

Sitting on the blanket, her legs tugged underneath her, Nora watched them. Matt was teaching Nat to swim and she wondered at his patience.

She hadn't heard him raise his voice once. Sounds carried on the lake and she heard his patient instructions, repeating things several times. He never tired.

From farther away, Ariel's harsh replies to Max's words clashed with the quietness of the lake. Apparently, everything Max said rubbed Ariel the wrong way.

After almost an hour, Matt took Nat back to the shore. The boy still had energy, but Matt knew he needed to have his afternoon snack.

They returned to the others and Nora noticed the food on the tables had been refreshed. New things had appeared, and her mouth watered when her eyes fell on the famous pastries both Marjorie and Bryan had baked. Apparently, a quiet competition was going on between the two of them.

Lily had already filled her plate with everything in sight. Nora suspected Lily's metabolism was very fast. She'd seen her eating and she couldn't have been so slender otherwise.

Nora smiled until her eyes fell on the cup with hot chocolate, which Lily had left on the table. Her eyes widened when she saw the tea spoon stirring the liquid. Lily didn't handle the spoon, and that shocked her.

Nora gasped and blinked hard. Matt immediately noticed what she'd seen and grumbled, "Lily."

Lily looked their way and suddenly, the tea spoon stopped moving. Nora looked from the spoon to Lily, and then to Matt who pretended to watch his brother, who was teasing Alex. She thought she'd imagined things and decided to let the matter drop.

"I might have a sunstroke," she said in a faltering voice.

She couldn't find any other explanation for what she'd witnessed. She rubbed her eyes with shaky fingers.

Matt took her hand, kissed it, and then said, "Let's take you to the shadow, all right. I'll fill a plate for you with everything," he assured her and spread the blanket under a tree.

He helped her sit, and, to his astonishment, he discovered he could read her thoughts and feel her turmoil now. He'd tried to read some of her thoughts during the last few weeks and couldn't.

Matt probed her mind a little, happy to be able to do it. Then, he blocked her thoughts, feeling like a voyeur.

He shook his head, overwhelmed with the significance of the event, and, after making sure she was comfortable, he returned to the food with Nat, to fill plates for all of them.

Nora still looked suspicious, unsure she'd imagined things or not. However, her rational mind didn't allow her to dwell on such impossible things. Probably, Lily had stirred her hot chocolate before, and inertia pushed the tea spoon to move. *'This is the only reasonable explanation'*, Nora nodded, and decided to leave it well alone.

CHAPTER EIGHTEEN

Everybody gathered on blankets, close enough to carry a conversation. They talked about everything and nothing.

Marjorie mentioned a few fundraisers she organized, and everyone offered their time and money to help out. Apparently, Matt's mother was a good organizer and she chose the neediest causes to support.

Ariel spoke about a few experiments she'd made with grafting some different species of plants. She was passionate about horticulture, yet, she didn't like her present job. She felt smothered and unchallenged. Nora understood she'd have liked to have a nursery one day.

Becka spoke about her classes and Bryan seemed to know everything about. Nora couldn't believe such attentive husbands existed. In her experience, men were egocentric and narcissistic.

Everyone shared something and they tried to make her share as well, but she didn't have anything to share.

She was afraid to let them know about how things had evolved with Matt and nothing else had happened in her life lately. She just recounted something Nat had done and they seemed to be content with that.

After a while, they broke into groups and moved a little farther. Becka, Ariel, Maggie and Lily were playing with the babies and entertained Nat.

The older generation gathered on one blanket and shared their concerns about their children in hushed voices. Yet, now and then, something reached Nora's ears, and she wondered why all of them seemed concerned about a specific task the young people had to complete. She intended to ask Matt later, hoping he wouldn't mind her nosiness.

The men started playing football. Just Matt remained with her, always holding her in his arms and whispering some nonsense words in her ear.

The afternoon trailed along. The sun was bright and a light breeze ruffled Nora's hair. Everything was just perfect.

She might have dozed for a while, lulled to sleep by Matt's endearments and the heat coming from his body. She breathed the salty smell of his skin, and her body reacted immediately. Yet, she still fell asleep.

When she woke up, her eyes searched for Nat immediately, and she smiled when she found him. He was still with the women and the babies.

Maggie played hocus-pocus for children and Nora had to admit she was very good at it. She'd produced a little bird out of thin air, and Nat almost laughed his heart out. Then she snapped her fingers, and a small chocolate bar appeared in her hand. She handed it to Nat and he looked at her adoringly.

Nora was in awe. She'd seen shows before, but Maggie was smoother than any other magician she'd seen. As a rule, Nora could guess how they did what they did, but there was no way to say with Maggie.

Nat turned to Ariel and said something, and Ariel smiled. She snapped her fingers and a red apple appeared in her palm.

Nora frowned in confusion. The apple was big and she didn't see where Ariel could have hidden it. She still wore her swimsuit only. Just a few moments ago, Nora had wondered how Ariel didn't melt under Max's hot stare. The man's eyes zeroed in on her and he practically didn't blink.

The baby in Lily's arms raised his arms, and the toys on the blanket beneath them floated in the air.

That was too much. Scared now, Nora jumped out of Matt's embrace and shouted, "What the heck's going on here?"

Her words stopped all activities. Even the men, who were playing football, forgot about the ball, which kept rolling to the edge of the water. No one paid any attention when it went under the surface of the lake.

Nora felt all eyes were on her, but now, she didn't care. She was scared. She couldn't find any reasonable explanations to what she'd seen and her fear escalated. Her chest heaved. She was breathing hard and her head felt light. Then, she fainted.

"Damn," Matt grumbled, and rushed to catch her.

"I am sorry," Becka said, coming toward them.

Bryan followed her with his eyes, and then asked Max to follow him inside the house.

Max understood something was happening and his friend didn't want him to witness it. He respected Bryan too much not to heed his call.

Becka sat on Matt's blanket, and stroked Nora's hair.

"I still can't stop the babies whenever they choose to play," she explained to Matt. "Sean has just discovered he can move objects. Imagine how titillating it is for him," she apologized. "They're too young to understand when they may do some things and when they shouldn't. I imagine it will take a few years…"

"Don't worry, sweetie," Matt said. "She had to find out somehow. She's a very rational woman and I'd have had a hard time to make her belief if she hadn't witnessed everything by herself," he pointed out.

He brushed his lips over Nora's, and then, whispered, "Come on, Nora, come back, baby. Wake up."

After a couple of attempts, Nora opened her eyes. Confusion glimmered in her green pupils, and her eyes searched Matt's face for an answer. She sat up in his arms, rubbed her eyes, and then turned to him.

"I think I'm hallucinating, Matt," she confessed with a small voice. She still sounded scared.

Matt shook his head, his eyes on her face.

"What do you mean?" she asked breathlessly.

"You aren't hallucinating," he answered very matter-of-factly.

"Impossible, Matt. Do you know what I thought I saw?"

"Not really, but I can imagine. Although, if you give me a second, and allow me to read your mind, I can answer."

All color disappeared from Nora's face. Her lips quivered and her fingers shook on Matt's forearm.

"What do you mean?"

"I mean I can read your thoughts, baby, but I won't do it if you don't allow me," he answered quietly.

She scowled at him for a second, and then she taunted him, "All right, read away."

He looked at her intently for a few seconds, and then chuckled.

"First of all, I didn't know you had such a colorful vocabulary, Nora," he jokingly chastised her. Then, he became serious, "Right now, you're thinking I'm playing with you, but in the back of your mind you still wonder what's going on. I understand you saw Sean lifting the toys off the blanket, Nora. It's no big deal," he started to say, but she interrupted him.

"What do you mean it's no big deal, Matthew Winston?" she asked in a very strong voice. "And how come you knew what I was thinking?" she thought to ask when the reality dawned on her.

"What Sean did is called telekinesis. If someone has the gift, it is no big deal. So far, Becka, Lily, Alex, Josh and now Sean have that gift," Matt explained, and her eyes widened in shock.

"What Maggie and Ariel did?" she remembered their exploits and asked in a fearful voice.

"That's just... witchcraft," Matt said and winced, imagining how that would sound in her ears.

She pushed away from him, scrambled a little farther and stared at him. Then, she looked around at everyone.

"What do you mean?" she bellowed now.

"Well, I'd say..." Matt started to say, but Alex beat him to the punch.

"Come on, Matt, you're a wuss. Things are simple, Nora," he turned to her, although Matt tried to stop him.

"We're witches. Well, most of us. My mother isn't, Matt's father and Becka's mother aren't, and, of course, Bryan. The rest of us inherited several talents. Some have one talent, others have two or three. Some of us cultivated them, and others didn't. That's all," he shrugged.

Nora just looked at him at a loss of words. She couldn't accept what he said.

"What?" she inquired, dizzy already.

"By God, Matt, you said she's a smart woman," Alex grumbled with disgust.

"Shut up," Matt bellowed at him. "And leave, now."

He was furious with his cousin. He didn't have any tact at all and he didn't care if he insulted anyone.

Marjorie came to Nora and took her hand.

"Pumpkin, it's not like we're a horrible family. We just have a few gifts, that's all. There are people who can play an instrument. I can do automatic writing and read people emotions, for instance. Matt can read minds and emotions and so on, Nora. It's nothing to be afraid of. Ask Jonathan, if you want. We've been married for thirty-seven years now, and he's never had anything to fear. Right, Jonathan?" she turned to her husband.

Jonathan approached her. He took Marjorie's hand and kissed it. Now Nora knew where Matt had learned to do that.

"I had only one fear, my love," he said, a whimsical smile on his lips. "That I won't give you the happiness you deserve."

Marjorie's eyes shimmered with joyful tears. She turned back to Nora, patted her shoulder and said, "You'll see you have nothing to worry about. Just think of what you know of Matt, and you'll do the right choice, pumpkin, I'm sure of that."

Nora stubbornly looked away, and Matt sighed.

"I think we should go back home," he suggested, and everybody agreed.

They started to pick up everything, when Nat came to Matt and asked, "What's a witch, Matt?"

Nora froze in place.

CHAPTER NINETEEN

Nora felt frozen inside. The cruise over the lake didn't calm her, as it had happened before. When Matt transferred everything in his car, she just waited aside, her thoughts churning in her head.

Everyone came to say their good-byes, but she seemed aloof, and they didn't linger.

Matt helped her in the car, after he secured Nat in the child's chair in the back. He leaned over her and locked her seatbelt, when he noticed she just stared through the windshield.

Suddenly, she turned her eyes onto him, and said, "I want to go home."

"We're going home," Matt nodded quietly.

Her hand grabbed his, and she said through tight teeth, "My home, not yours."

He shook his head, and instinctively, leaned over her and kissed her hard.

"I'm sorry, sweetheart, I can't drive you to your apartment. You're not hundred percent, and you can't take care of yourself and Nat the right way," he denied her requests, shaking his head.

When he saw she wanted to interrupt him, he touched his fingers to her mouth, shaking his head again.

"I know you'll try, Nora. You're strong and stubborn enough to try. But your body won't let you. I have to take you home with me," he repeated mulishly, and the tone of his voice didn't leave room for arguments.

"I won't sleep with you," she lashed out at him.

He remained still, hurt visible in his eyes, but then, he nodded, "All right, you'll sleep in the other bedroom, if that's what you want."

"That's what I want," she replied meanly. "You lied to me and…"

"I've never lied to you," he answered quietly. "I just haven't revealed everything."

With those words, he closed her car door and jogged to the other side to get them home.

The drive home didn't take more than five minutes. When they got upstairs, Nora wanted to take Nat with her in the empty bedroom, but Nat didn't understand why he couldn't spend the remaining of the afternoon with Matt, and started crying.

Emotionally exhausted, she left them alone and left. Regardless everything, she still trusted Matt to take care of her son.

Lying in bed, she kept turning things in her head. The shock hadn't worn off yet, and she still couldn't believe the Watsons were witches. She knew there wasn't such a thing as witches.

She considered paranormal abilities, although, in the past, she discounted them. She still didn't reach any conclusion, and, after a while, worn out, she fell asleep.

Matt's fingers, skimming over her face, woke Nora. She blinked and looked at him confused. He'd turned on the lamp on the night table, and she realized it was already dark outside.

"Hey, there," he said softly. "I didn't know whether I should let you sleep. It's late though, and you haven't had any dinner yet. Do you want me to bring it here or do you think you could stand having dinner with me?"

His eyes showed his insecurity, and her heart cringed. Matt was a kind man and she didn't want to hurt him. However, she couldn't just gloss over what had happened.

"I could have something to eat," she mumbled.

"Do you want me to bring you a tray here?" he offered again.

"No," she replied sitting up. "I'll be in the kitchen in a couple of minutes."

"Do you need my help for anything?" he asked, straightening up.

"I'm pretty sure I can go to the bathroom under my own steam, Matt," she answered back. "I don't need your paranormal powers to support me."

Her voice sounded spiteful. She felt cruel and raw and she didn't feel like cutting him any slack.

Matt took in her bad mood, nodded, and left the room, locking his hands at the back of his head.

The feeling of defeat was gnawing at him, and he didn't know how to stop that train wreck.

***

When Nora came into the living-room, Matt was seated at the breakfast table, watching the lake. He'd already laid everything out on the table.

Sensing her arrival, he turned to her and stood up. *Always the consummated gentleman,* she thought, and then, she chided herself. Matt had always been considerate and respectful, and she was just lashing at him now, because of what she'd uncovered that afternoon.

She moseyed to the table and sat down. Matt held her chair and then, he took his seat again.

He started serving her with salad first, and then, he added a large grilled chicken breast and stir-fried vegetables on her plate. Always in silence, he filled his plate and with a gesture invited her to eat.

They ate in complete silence for a few minutes, and then, Nora looked up at him and asked, "Did you intend to ever let me know?"

"Yes," he answered.

She didn't like his brief answer, and scowled at him.

"Yeah? When? Sometime in the next twenty or thirty years?"

She sounded like a shrew, and Matt's left eyebrow hiked up his forehead. She blushed slightly, but her expression didn't change.

"Actually, no, Nora. I knew I had to let you know before we'd become more involved."

"Really?" she asked mockingly. "How more involved should we have been for you to spill the beans?"

His eyes turned hard. Matt had hoped they could discuss things reasonably, without attacking each other.

He understood she felt betrayed somehow. He didn't try to read her mind. He didn't feel he had the right of doing it without her knowledge. But her emotions were very strong, and no empathic person could have stopped the emotional waves.

"Definitely, before taking you into my bed and before asking you to be my wife," he replied silently.

To mask his concerns, he cut a piece of chicken and stuffed it in his mouth. He didn't taste it, but chewed carefully before swallowing.

Nora's eyes widened and a faint blush colored the top of her cheeks. Her fingers shook on the fork, which clanked on the plate. The sound resonated in their ears and she put the fork down. She leaned back and measured him.

"You've already taken me into your bed," Nora observed with sarcasm.

"Not the way I want to," Matt replied with a shrug. "I love cuddling with you, and I need sleeping with you," he admitted. "But I do need much more than that."

"I see," she said quietly and crossed her arms over her chest.

Nora looked at him a little more, and then said, "You know you could have had something more for some time now."

"Maybe," he shrugged again and forked some vegetables. "Eat your food, Nora, it's getting cold."

"How, the heck, do you think I can eat now?" she scowled at him.

"The same way I do," he replied, and nodded his head toward her plate to nudge her to eat.

"I'm not as insensible as you are," she said through her teeth, and Matt stilled.

She realized what she said, and recalling how careful and attentive Matt had been with her, she wanted to slap herself silly.

Nora reached out and touched Matt's hand, "I'm sorry, Matt. You don't deserve that. I'm just very upset and scared, you know."

"I can imagine," he groused.

"No," she replied with a self-deprecating laugh, "you can read my mind. You don't have to imagine anything."

"Actually, I do, Nora. As I said, I'll never read your mind without permission. Your emotions though…"

"What about them?" she inquired.

"I can't block them. I'll always know what you feel. I mean I know if you're happy or sad, or if you're scared or hurt, you know. I don't know if you love or hate someone… I'd have to read your mind for that," he explained to her, and waved his hand to her, again, inviting her to eat.

This time, Nora took her fork and played around with her vegetables, pensively.

"When you didn't allow me to play cards with Jay," she said and looked up at him, "was it because of his talents?"

Matt nodded and continued to chew. It took him a few seconds to swallow.

He reached out to her and interlocked their fingers. Then, he turned her hand, palm up, and his thumb started drawing circles on her smooth skin.

Nora felt his caress everywhere inside her body and swallowed hard.

"Yes, Jay has extra sensorial perception, ESP, if you want. He can see what cards you have in your hand. For the moment, he can't really control the gift and as result, he can't stop using it. Playing cards with him is... a farce, if you want," Matt shrugged.

"I see," Nora, said. "Outside the family, does anyone else know what you can do? I mean you and your cousins... you understand what I mean."

"No," Matt answered. "There are people who'd consider us freaks. Others would want to take advantage of what we can do. So, no, only the people in the family know about. Of course, the ones marrying into the family are told beforehand so they could choose... So far," he said in a very soft voice, "none of them backed out."

They looked at each other intently.

"You said," Nora started in an hesitant voice, "that you wanted to have me in your bed and marry me."

"Yes, I do. Both," Matt nodded.

"Why me?" she asked, and Matt blinked.

"Come again?" he asked confused.

"Why me? Why would you want to marry me?" she repeated more forcefully. "Because I found out what the Winstons can do?"

"Don't be stupid," he replied in a harsh voice. "I wouldn't marry for such a trivial reason, Nora."

"Then why me?" she repeated stubbornly. "Why would you be interested in marrying me?"

His eyes rounded, and the intensity of the dark blue took her breath away. Matt shook his head and stood up to pace, lost in thought.

After a few minutes, he came back to her.

"I can't understand. You're a smart woman. I've seen proof of your intelligence in many occasions. How can such a smart woman ask such stupid questions?" he asked, shaking his head.

"Look here," she stood at her turn. "I'm not stupid."

"That I know," he agreed with her. "I don't know how you can't see it, though."

"See what?" Nora asked with exasperation.

"That I love you," Matt replied.

He registered the shock on her face. Nora fell back on her chair looking at him with disbelief.

"Yeah, I can see you're crushed with joy," he said dryly.

He took his plate and the platters on the table into the kitchen. He cleaned them and put them into the dishwasher. She was still watching him with incredulity.

"Finish your dinner, Nora," he invited her, quietly. "Leave everything on the table. I'll take care of the dishes later. Good night," he added and left the room.

Nora remained at the table, looking out of the window, yet her eyes didn't register anything. On one hand, Matt's words elated her. On the other, they scared her, because she didn't know whether she loved him too.

Late, she realized her food was cold and her body stiff, because she'd been sitting in the same position for too long. With difficulty, she stood and slowly made her way to her room.

CHAPTER TWENTY

Nora was sitting on the window sill bench, watching the lake, when the intercom beeped. She grimaced and abandoned her place to answer the door.

Being Canada Day, Matt had taken Nat to see some shows on Harbor Front, together with Marjorie and Becka.

Although she had some apprehensions about the abilities running in the Winston family, she trusted Matt and his family with her son.

The last two weeks had been awkward. Matt had always been polite, but withdrawn. She'd been reserved.

They took their meals together, and Matt took Nat to visit Becka and Bryan regularly. They went together in the park, but Nora always refused to go out.

She didn't know how to react around Matt anymore. She knew she'd been mean and spiteful and she didn't know how to take her words back. Her former marriage had left her unprepared to fix the situation.

Nora was exhausted. Her mind churned around her feelings for Matt and what he'd told her.

She also worried about returning back to her apartment. As she suspected, her disability pay covered the rent, and she had only about two hundred dollars left in the bank after paying it.

She could solve that problem only if she'd returned to work, which seemed out of the question. The doctor didn't want to sign off. She had asked him just that when she had her medical appointment the other day, and he refused.

Yet, she knew she couldn't take advantage of Matt anymore. He was surly now, and she assumed he allowed her to stay in his apartment just because of his chivalrous up-bringing.

Nora pushed the button to the intercom and unlocked the door without asking who it was. She didn't really care. Her loneliness had become so acute that she'd have welcomed anyone, even Alex, who didn't seem to like her much.

When she heard the knock on the door, she opened it immediately and found herself before Bryan.

She sketched a shy smile and waved him to come inside. She knew she'd feel awkward to see someone after the fiasco at the lake, but she didn't expect to feel so bad.

Bryan entered, watching her carefully. He leaned over and kissed her cheek.

"You seem awfully tired and depressed," he noticed. "Is everything fine?"

"You flatter me, Bryan" she replied dryly.

"Not my intention, Nora," he shook his head. "I've brought something for us," he told her, showing the bag in his hand. "Go and take a sit on the sofa. I'll put everything on a platter and come to join you."

"I can put everything on the platter," she replied stubbornly, and snatched the bag. "Now, you can go and sit on the sofa," she said and give him a push in the direction of the sofa.

Bryan didn't budge at first, then he laughed, put his hands up to show he surrendered, and sauntered to the sofa. He could see Nora in the kitchen, trying to locate the platters.

He chuckled and told her, "Try the last cupboard down on the left. That's where Matt keeps the platters. He still doesn't let you in the kitchen, I see," he observed.

"You know he doesn't," she replied ruefully. "Either you or Marjorie provide the food. I'm not allowed to do anything around here and it drives me crazy," she confessed, arranging the pastries on the platter.

"Have you told him that?" Bryan inquired mildly, always watching her, judging her reactions and emotions.

Nora shrugged, but said nothing. She carried the platter to the coffee table and asked, "Would you like some coffee, coke or beer?"

"A beer would be good," he answered with a shrug. "Don't bother with a glass, Nora. I don't need one," he thought to mention. He never bothered about etiquette.

She returned to the kitchen to bring him the beer, and he noticed with satisfaction that she moved easier. She wasn't completely healed, and from what Matt had told him, he knew she might remain with a slight limp for her entire life, which didn't bother Matt at all.

It was important that she was on the road of recovery. Now, only if he could help to heal her other wounds.

Nora returned with a beer for him and a coke for her. She sat in an armchair and sighed.

"Tough day?" Bryan inquired.

"Tough couple of months," she replied with a nod.

"I can see that. So, why haven't you told Matt that you'd like to do some work in the kitchen?"

She looked away. Then, she leaned forward and picked a piece of pastry.

"You're avoiding my question," Bryan observed.

"Of course, I'm avoiding your question," she snapped at him.

"Why?" he insisted.

She sighed deeply, and then, she gave in.

"Because Matt and I are not really talking, you know. He asks if I'm okay and if I want to eat something or watch a movie. He asks permission for taking Nat with him... But nothing else," she shrugged.

"Since when?"

"Like you don't know," she scowled at Bryan. "Since that blasted day at your lake house."

"So, you're upset with Matt for what had happened there and what you found out," he concluded.

"I was. Then," she thought to specify. "Come on, Bryan, don't tell me you wouldn't have been surprised if something like that had happened to you," she lifted her eyebrows in disbelief.

Bryan shouted with laughter and slapped his knee. His eyes sparked with amusement.

"What's so funny?" Nora frowned, not understanding how he could laugh in such circumstances.

"You, Nora, you're funny."

"Because I was surprised and scared when all that happened?" she asked with dismay.

Actually, she hadn't expected that coarse behavior from Bryan. He didn't seem the kind of man to make fun of someone just for the sake of it. *'How wrong can I be sometimes,'* she thought.

"Of course not. I wouldn't laugh at you for that, Nora," he scowled at her.

He'd hoped she knew him better by then.

"I'm laughing because you assume I've never been in that position," he hooted again, shaking his head.

Nora just looked at him, her eyebrows up her forehead. She'd never seen Bryan in such a state.

"Imagine," he said, "I took Becka exactly to the same spot. We made love for the first time, one of the most beautiful moments in my life, by the way. And then we quarreled," he said. "You'll certainly hear why," he added with a wave of his hand. "I won't waste our time going into those details.

Pretty soon, someone will find a great joy relating the events to you. I've been the butt of their jokes ever since," he flapped his hand with disgust. "Anyway, at the time, I didn't know anything about her family and, to be perfectly honest with you, I didn't believe in such things," he explained.

"I know what you mean," Nora said. "I had the same ideas and everything came as a shock."

"Yes, I know. It was the same with me. Anyway, at the time, Becka couldn't control her powers, you know. She got so upset with me that the wind started gushing around us, and things flew into the air," he shook his head, chuckling. "Imagine, a big cooler just flying around, past your head. Oh, boy, that did scare me," he confessed, although he was laughing.

Nora listened to him with astonishment.

"What did you do?" she asked breathlessly. She'd have run for cover and waited there until the coast would have been clear.

Bryan ran his fingers through his hair, gulped from his beer, and then, looking straight into her eyes, said, "I was an ass. The biggest possible ass. I treated her as if she'd been a freak. I hurt her, and deeply."

"Oh, my God. How did she accept you back?" Nora asked wide-eyed. She wouldn't have been able to forgive something like that.

"I was lucky, I think. I went by her house a few days after. I had in mind to beg, grovel... You know -- do everything possible to make her forgive me. But she forgave me immediately. She didn't feel the need to punish me."

"I see," Nora murmured, yet she found hard to believe that a woman could just push something like that aside and forget about it.

"Now, let me tell you something, Nora. If I could accept things flying around and winds and storms, believe me, you can accept Matt's talent. His, at least, doesn't scare you. You know he can't hurt you. Like by hitting your head with a cooler, for instance," Bryan said, laughing.

"Matt has asked you to come and talk to me," she concluded, clenching her hands together.

"Oh, no, Nora. Don't even tell him I talked to you about this. He'd skin me first. I'd love to remain in good relations with Matt. He's one of the good guys, you know. I don't want to lose his friendship, Nora. But I know he pines over you, and if I were to guess after seeing you today, you pine over him too. Why don't you cut a slack to both of you, and try to talk to him? I understand he's afraid you don't want to listen to what he has to say and he hurts," Bryan said, finishing off his beer.

"I'd like to talk to him, but I don't even know where to begin. I'm also afraid he'd think I'm only trying to take advantage of him because of my present situation and that's the worse," she confessed, leaning forward. "He knows the doctor won't sign me off for work and I'm in a bad financial situation."

"Then just give him permission to read your mind. That should banish any kind of doubts and suspicions. I assure you, the process is painless, I tried it," Bryan said in a matter-of-fact voice.

"Easy for you to say," she snapped.

"I know it's easy for me to say," Bryan nodded. "It's always easy to give advice, I know. But if you don't do something, you'll both lose. Matt won't ever pressure you. And if he thinks that's what you want, he'll leave you alone, no matter how much he hurts," Bryan explained to her.

Nora closed her eyes and bit her bottom lip. Bryan could almost see the little wheels turning, round and round.

"May I ask something more from you, Bryan?" Nora suddenly opened her eyes and trained her shiny green eyes on him.

"Of course, you can," Bryan nodded.

"Would Becka and you keep Nat over the night? Today or maybe tomorrow, if you can't today," she rushed to say.

"We can keep him with us today, not a problem. It will be fun," he grinned. "Let me call Becka and tell her. She's with Matt and Nat right now. She can take Nat directly home, and you and Matt can have the apartment to yourself tonight," Bryan winked at her and took his phone out of his pocket.

He dialed Becka's number and explained everything as fast as possible, warning her from the beginning not to say a thing to Matt.

CHAPTER TWENTY-ONE

Matt dreaded an entire afternoon and evening alone with Nora. He longed to be with her, and yet, knowing she didn't want to talk to him, simply made his chest ache.

Becka had asked to have Nat with her until the next day. She assured him she'd cleared it with Nora.

He still checked with Nora, and that made Becka growl at him, which cheered Nat considerably.

They were just about to go home and the boy didn't really want to go inside. He'd have preferred to run along the harbor.

Marjorie had wanted to accompany Matt at home. He'd sensed it. Yet, Becka took her hand and invited her to see the twins.

Matt couldn't compete with the twins those days. Soon, his mother sauntered to Becka's car and left with her.

Matt resigned himself to another afternoon of silence. The thought that Nora was in the same apartment with him, so close, and yet, so far away, killed him slowly.

He groaned, but he didn't have anything else to do. He drove back home.

To his dismay, he didn't encounter any traffic stops, any traffic jams, anything. He got there in no time. With a sigh, he parked his car and leaned his head on the driving wheel for a few seconds.

'Start cracking, scaredy-cat,' he mumbled and got out of the car.

His apartment was on the twenty-seventh floor, and sometimes, the trip by elevator seemed to take forever. Of course, not that day. It felt as if the elevator had transported him to his floor in the blink of an eye.

He headed to his door with dread. He breathed deeply, preparing himself for another silent treatment, and then unlocked the door.

As expected, the apartment was silent. He knew she wouldn't welcome him, as she'd done in the past.

Suddenly, a painful thought popped into his head. Nora had left, and her request to Becka was just a decoy. She'd be waiting for Nat at Becka's house, and head with him to her own apartment afterward.

"No," he bellowed, and his fist punched the wall with all the force he was capable.

Matt wanted his chance and he couldn't just lie down and have it slip through his fingers. He couldn't let Nora go without a word.

He practically tore the door down when he pulled it open. He didn't care his knuckles were bleeding or he might destroy the door.

He'd barely got out of the door with a purposeful stride, when Nora called him from behind, "Matt, where are you going? What's happened?"

Matt staggered on his feet. He slowly turned around, and his eyes fell squarely on Nora.

Wide-eyed, she looked from him to the hole in the wall and back. She paled when her eyes zeroed in on his bloody knuckles.

"That's what I heard," she whispered. "You punched the wall," she said louder, shaking her head.

She couldn't believe he'd done that. Matt was always calm and composed. He wasn't a hothead and she couldn't reconcile the image she had before her eyes with the Matt she knew.

She stared at him and bellowed, "Are you out of your mind? Why, the heck, would you do that?"

Matt flapped his hand, tried to say something, and then scowled at her. He didn't find the courage to admit why he'd done it.

"What's the matter? What made you so angry?" Nora asked again, in a calmer voice this time.

She'd have never thought there was anything that could make Matt lose his temper. He was constantly so patient and understanding that his present behavior astonished her.

'What made me so angry? The woman is clueless, damn it! She's just torn my heart apart and she's asking what's the matter,' Matt shook his head.

Then, he cleared his throat, looked away for a few seconds. Reaching a decision, he closed the door behind him. He threw the keys in the bowl on the table near the door, and only then, he looked back at her.

He felt stupid for what he'd done, and he knew he had to say something and explain his behavior. Lying to Nora wasn't a choice.

"I thought you left," he said with a sigh.

"I beg your pardon?" she replied, wide-eyed.

"I thought you left the apartment. You left me," he repeated, "and you asked Becka to take Nat, so you could go to her house and take him with you," he explained louder, his tone of voice rebellious.

He sounded like a petulant child explaining why he'd done a stupid thing. For a few seconds, Nora couldn't answer. Her green eyes showed bewilderment at first, and then anger.

"Really? Do you really think I'd be so callous, Matt?" Nora asked, hardly keeping her temper in check.

He sensed his words had offended her and tried to apologize, "I'm sorry, baby. I didn't think. I just reacted," he opened his arms, at a loss of words. He didn't know what to say and make her hurt less.

"You should know me better than that," she said, morosely.

"I know you better," he admitted. "I've just lost my common sense for a moment."

Nora looked him over, and then, she took his hand and pulled him after her.

"Where are we going?" he asked, and again slapped himself in his mind for asking stupid questions. As long as she wanted him with her, he didn't mind where they were going.

She turned her head toward him and smiled, "Just in the living-room for the moment. Right after we've cleaned those knuckles and stopped the bleeding," she thought to add.

"The bleeding's stopped, don't worry about it," Matt waved the matter away, as unimportant.

"Come on, Matt, humor me. Let's clean those knuckles first, and we'll see afterward."

Matt gave in and let her fuss over his knuckles. When she finished, she led him into the living-room, and invited him to sit on the sofa. Satisfied that he was doing her bidding, she moseyed to the kitchen.

"By the way, Bryan passed by this afternoon," she said disappearing into the kitchen. "He brought some pastries for us. I asked him first if Nat could go to their house for a sleepover, and then he called Becka," her voice came from the kitchen and Matt leaned sideways, to see her through the alcove.

"Why did he come?" he asked, and suspicion rang in his voice.

Nora returned with a tray in her hands, and Matt immediately jumped to his feet and rushed to relieve her of the burden.

She tapped her foot on the floor furiously.

"I'm not frail, Matt Winston. I'm able to carry a tray," she grumbled at him.

"No, baby, you're not frail. But you won't carry a tray before another month or two. We'll see how it goes," he shrugged, without promising anything.

"With you, I won't be allowed to carry anything for the rest of my life," she glared at him, putting her hands on her hips.

Matt shrugged, and grinned at her. He was smart enough not to go into an argument with her right then.

"Come on, here, have a sit," he invited her, laying the platter on the coffee table in front of the sofa.

Nora decided to choose her battles and let that one go. She didn't see she'd win it anytime soon.

She sat on the sofa and, leaving her slippers on the floor, she tugged her legs under her. She leaned forward to take one of the plates on the tray and a pastry, but Matt immediately stopped her and prepared a plate for her. She huffed, but didn't comment.

She waited until Matt also helped himself to a pastry and sat in an armchair, not far from her.

During the last couple of weeks before the event at the lake, he'd bought two more armchairs and a few ottomans and pillows, he'd spread through the living-room.

It seemed necessary. They'd had guests almost every day at that time. They used to come in groups, and always commented on the lack of enough furniture.

After her melt-down at the lake, the group visits ended, and some visits stopped completely. Probably, people were wary of her.

"I think we should talk," she said, after biting into the pastry.

Matt was about to carry his pastry to the mouth, and his hand froze in mid-movement. His eyes darkened, and he didn't dare to blink.

"You don't need to worry," she said, with a small smile. "Or better said, I hope you won't worry. You said you could read my mind, if I allowed it," she continued in an inquiring voice.

Matt just nodded. He put the pastry back onto the plate and left the plate on the table.

"I allow it," she said softly. "Knock yourself out," she tried to lighten the mood, but Matt didn't feel so relieved.

"Are you sure?" he asked falteringly.

She nodded with determination and closed her eyes. She didn't know what reading her mind involved, but she'd already decided to take Bryan's advice and didn't want to back out.

Matt stared at her, and then, seeing that she didn't change her mind, closed his eyes and let himself immerse in her thoughts. He didn't need more than a few seconds to have tears in his eyes.

He left the armchair, and pulled her in his arms, forgetting about his earlier worries, and hugged her tight, until she said a soft *'ouch'*.

"Oh, baby, I am so sorry. I didn't mean to hurt you," he said in a rush and pulled himself at a distance.

"I know, Matt. You just held me too tight. Otherwise, you, touching me, that's not a problem," she said, and touched his face with her fingers, tracing his stubby beard.

Nora closed the distance between them, and slid her arms around him. She leaned her head on his chest, and breathed contentedly.

Matt hugged her again, not so tight this time, and kissed the top of her head.

"I'm ready now," she whispered.

Matt became so still, she feared he'd stopped breathing.

She looked up at him. She felt as if the intensity of his eyes had swallowed her. The dark-blue of his pupils turned darker.

"Do you mean, you're ready for me?" he asked, unsure of himself.

"Yes, if you haven't changed your mind, of course," she replied.

In a second, he scooped her up in his arms, and with huge strides headed to his bedroom.

"Not in this lifetime, Nora. Sorry, baby, not in this lifetime."

Once in his bedroom, he laid her on his bed and stepped back. He just stared at her, happy to see her lying in his bed once more.

Then, he turned back and closed the door, as if he'd been afraid the world would intrude upon them.

CHAPTER TWENTY-TWO

When they arrived at Marjorie's house, Nora couldn't believe her eyes. Her future mother-in-law hadn't spared any expenses.

Flowers covered every corner and every surface available. The buffet was decadent and in an array of colors that caught people's eye and watered their mouths.

Matt held her hand and chuckled at her surprise.

"Mom always knows how to give a party, baby," he brushed his lips on her cheek.

"I can see that," she replied in awe. "I've never seen anything like that. But she needn't have gone to so much trouble…" she shook her head.

"Honey, you have to understand something," Matt whispered in her ear. "I'm her first born. She's been waiting for this moment for thirty-four years. We must let her have her way," he advised, and Nora nodded.

Nat, who was holding her other hand, shouted, "Mommy, look, Becka's here."

Immediately, he pulled his hand out of hers and ran to Becka, his most favorite person in the world after Nora and Matt.

Becka welcomed him with a tight hug and a kiss on the cheek.

"Wow, you look so handsome," she praised him.

Matt had refused to have him dressed in a suit for the party. He'd insisted he was a child and needed to feel free to move around.

In the end, a compromise had been reached between all parties involved – Nat wouldn't wear a suit for the engagement party thrown by Marjorie for them, but he would wear one for the wedding.

Once the word they had arrived spread out, everybody came to congratulate them. Marjorie and Jonathan beamed with pride, and hugged both Nora and Matt several times.

People admired Nora's dress, and she blushed. Matt had weakened her resolve with a constant attack for a week and made her accept it. He bought it himself, and presented it to her as a gift, together with all the necessary accessories.

The emerald sleeveless silky dress hugged her body, without being snug. It stopped just at her knees. Her eyes shone stronger, reflecting the color of the dress.

Considerate, Matt bought low-heel shoes for her, so she wouldn't overtax her leg, and a small bag. He was already concerned she'd overdo it during the party, and he'd lectured her about not standing for too long and let him know when she got tired. By the end of the lecture, she'd rolled her eyes several times, but she promised to let him know if it became too much for her.

She remembered what Marjorie had said, about giving a man his due. Matt was always attentive and attuned to her needs. The least she could do was to respect his wishes in that concern.

They moseyed through the guests, holding hands, chatting about inconsequential things and answering questions.

They had to go different ways when men took him aside to discuss the bachelor's party, which he'd initially refused.

Nora had convinced him to accept it. It was like a coming to age ritual and she didn't want him to miss out on anything.

She went outside onto the patio with Lily for some fresh air. Marjorie had outdone herself, but Nora still felt smothered in large crowds.

"I understand the wedding will be at Bryan's house on the lake," Lily said, sipping from her glass with champagne, and eying Nora's dress.

That color would have worked for her too, but she needed it in another model. She didn't have Nora's curves.

"Yes," Nora smiled at her. "Becka will be my matron of honor, you know. We decided to have only a matron of honor and a best man. Otherwise, we wouldn't have had any guests or almost any," she laughed, and Lily shared her hilarity.

"Yep, you're right. I remember Becka's wedding. Only the old generation played the role of guests. We were all bridesmaids and groomsmen. It was hilarious," Lily giggled.

"What was hilarious?" Maggie sashayed to them, and toasted Nora.

"Becka's wedding," Lily explained. "With all of us part of the wedding party, remember?"

"Oh, yes," Maggie made a face. "I hope you won't do that to us," she implored Nora.

"Don't worry," Nora replied, laughing. "Just Becka and Bryan. Everyone else will be considered guest."

"Phew, thank God, Nora!"

She wiped off her forehead, theatrically, and the other two women laughed at her antics.

"So, I see you grabbed him, eventually," Rebecca's voice came from behind Nora.

Nora turned stiffly to the old woman. She hadn't seen Rebecca since the day when she came to the hospital. She couldn't say she'd missed her.

Rebecca sneered at her, and, suddenly, Lily turned on her heels and rushed to the house.

"Hello, Rebecca," Nora replied calmly. "I don't remember to have ever grabbed a man," she said and sipped unhurriedly from her glass.

She tried to hide any sign of distress. She knew Rebecca would pounce on her if she saw any weakness.

"Great-grandma," Maggie intervened in a bored voice, "I think Matt did all the grabbing, in the end. I can vouch for that, actually. I witnessed almost everything," she flapped her hand.

"I'm sure you have something else to do, young lady, so get lost," Rebecca snapped at her.

Maggie seemed to reflect a moment, then she shook her head, "No, sorry, grandma. Nothing to do. I was actually doing something," she pointed out. "I was talking to Nora. But it's not a problem," she patted her grandma's arm. "We can include you in our conversation. Right, Nora?" she asked and winked at Nora, who couldn't stop a crooked smile in the corner of her mouth.

"Girl, your manners are lacking," Rebecca snapped at Maggie again. "You don't know when you're not wanted somewhere. Now, get lost."

"Actually, Nora wants me here, don't you, Nora?"

Nora assessed the old woman before her eyes. Her annoyance with Maggie was escalating, and Nora didn't want to be the instrument of a rift between the two of them.

"It's okay, Maggie. Rebecca seems determined to tell me something, so we'd better let her do it. Meantime, would you mind filling me a plate with desserts? I saw them earlier and couldn't take my mind off them," she asked Maggie and stroked her arm.

"Are you sure?" Maggie asked unconvinced.

"Yes, I am," Nora replied, smiling.

Yet, Maggie read a fierce determination beyond that smile.

"All right, grandma, the scene is all yours," Maggie bowed mockingly, and Rebecca's eyes thundered at her.

Maggie glided toward the house, giggling.

Rebecca watched her leaving, and then turned to Nora. She stared her down with hard eyes, but then, Nora didn't back down either. She squared her shoulders and looked straight into Rebecca's eyes.

"Do you know you ruined all chances for Matthew?" Rebecca asked in a haughty voice.

"I don't know what you mean," Nora shook her head.

"He could have had everything," Rebecca threw her hands in the air.

Nora heard the sudden rustle of leaves and felt the gushes of cold air surrounding her. Her heart skipped a beat, remembering Bryan's story, but she told herself Rebecca couldn't kill her in Marjorie's house. She matched her look for look.

Rebecca scowled and threw her fist into the air. A black cloud appeared and rain started to pour over Nora.

Nora didn't move or show distress. *'A little rain didn't kill anyone'*, she thought.

Suddenly everyone was out on the patio. They were thundering at Rebecca, and Matt's voice was the loudest. He ran and hugged Nora to his chest.

"If you ever, and I mean ever, touch her, even with your thought, I won't recognize you as part of my family," he bit Rebecca's head off, and she gasped.

"You'd do that for her?" she asked with outrage.

"She's the woman I love. She'll be my wife in a week. You either respect her and my decisions and wishes, or you can forget I exist," he glowered, and took Nora with him.

Passing by his mother, who looked completely shocked, he asked in a mild voice, "Could you help Nora with something to wear, mother?"

She nodded and joined them on their way inside.

Everyone looked at Rebecca with astonished eyes. She'd been vocal in the past, but she never attacked anyone.

"Why?" Bryan asked her quietly. "You weren't so malevolent to me, and I, at least, did look like a ruffian," he said.

"Bryan," Becka shouted at him. "How dare you to speak like that about yourself?"

"Calm down, sweetheart. We need to know why she hates Nora," he stroked Becka's arms to soothe her.

"You hate my mommy?" Nat's voice interfered, and the grown-ups groaned.

"If Matt finds out he knows, it will be hell," Jonathan whispered to Amelie, who was closest to him.

Amelie immediately came forward and took Nat's hand. She said soothingly, "No one hates your mommy, Nat. You saw we all love her."

"But she doesn't," the boy said stubbornly.

"I don't hate her," Rebecca replied to the child. "I hate that plans were ruined, that's all," she said and tried to ruffle the child's hair, but Nat stepped back.

He looked at her for a few more seconds, and then looked up at Amelie, "May I have another slice of cake, auntie?"

Amelie nodded and smiled relieved that the crisis had been averted. She loved it when the boy called her auntie.

Nat had been told Matt would marry his mommy and, consequently, would become his daddy. That news made him happy. He already loved Matt, who always made time for him and never berated him.

Then, everyone told him to call them auntie or uncle, and, suddenly, he found himself in the middle of a huge family. More important, everyone tried to make him happy and paid attention to him.

***

Nora, Marjorie and Matt returned after fifteen minutes. Nora had refused a dress, but accepted a pair of pants and a shirt.

She had to explain to Matt several times that she didn't hold him responsible for what happened, and no, she didn't change her mind. She would marry him the following Saturday.

Matt was seething. He'd always known his grandma was a cold woman, who put her wishes and thoughts above everyone's. Yet, he'd never imagined she'd truly use her abilities to hurt someone, and especially the woman he loved.

Rebecca was still there when they arrived on the patio, and Matt simply saw red before his eyes. His stride lengthened, determined to get to her and throw her out, but Nora squeezed his fingers and, gently, pulled him back.

He looked at her over the shoulder, and she shuddered at the black intent in his gaze.

"No," she quietly said. "You won't do anything to tear your family apart."

"She hurt you," he growled.

"Not really. She just doused me," she shrugged. "It's no big deal, Matt. A little rain never killed anyone."

"I don't care," he barked again.

"But I do," she replied quietly, and he closed his eyes.

"All right, I won't throw her out, but she must not touch you. Ever."

She nodded, and both joined the others.

Rebecca pierced them with a black look. She fisted her hands and advanced toward Matt.

"You're making a mistake, Matt."

"It's mine to make," he replied in an icy voice. "And I don't see any mistake from where I stand," he pointed out.

"You won't get all your powers and your money," she snapped.

"Sorry to disappoint you, grandma, but I do have the powers. And the money… you know I have no reasons to complain," he snickered.

"You can't," she stepped back horrified. "You're with her just because you're a kind man and feel sorry for her."

"I told you not to insult her again," he started toward her with angry steps, but Nora, pulled his hand and he stopped.

"Nora, she's maligning you," he complained.

"So what?" she replied. "It's not like I care."

"But do you care you cost him his abilities and his money?" Rebecca asked her in a mean voice.

"What is she talking about, Matt?" Nora asked, a frown between her eyebrows. "Have you lost something because you're with me?" she raised her voice.

"No, baby, quite the opposite," he assured her. "Because of our love, I finally have all the abilities I was supposed to have."

"I don't understand," Nora complained.

"Let me explain," Bryan said, striding toward them, a smile in the corner of his mouth. "As an outsider, and once in your shoes, I might make more sense, Nora," he told her and came closer.

Rebecca gave him the evil eye, but he just smiled at her.

"You see, because of two tragedies in her life, great-grandma cursed all generations to come. They can't reach their full potential and use their abilities, until they've fallen in love and committed to someone," Bryan explained.

He stretched out his hand to Becka, and she immediately linked her fingers with his.

"For instance," he continued, "Matt's love for you helped him to control his mind reading skills and other extra sensorial perceptions," he said.

Nora looked at Matt, and he nodded, then leaned over her, kissed her lips and whispered, "You see, you brought me much more joy that I could have ever dreamed."

Nora blushed and Bryan chortled.

"Now, to continue, Nora. Rebecca also set up trust funds for her grandchildren, and later for her great-grandchildren. But they couldn't or can't get that money until they fall in love, commit to someone and that someone commits to them. Of course, there's a set of trustees – mind readers, you see, who can check if someone tries to cheat. I understand someone did, in the past," he chuckled, looking at Jay, who scowled at him.

"Why everyone has to bring me into this discussion?" he asked with disgust, throwing his hands into the air.

"Because your story is funny," Bryan answered, and winked at him.

"Then," Nora said hesitantly, "I don't see what Matt has lost by being with me."

She looked at Rebecca inquiringly and then at Matt.

"That's the idea, love. I lost nothing, but I got everything," he said and lifted her hand to his lips and kissed it.

"Yeah?" Rebecca snickered. "Then prove it."

"The only thing we have to do is prove it to each other, grandma," Matt shook his head. "We don't have to prove anything to you."

"You're afraid," she said with an ugly laugh. "You know the trustees will see through this sham, as I have already seen."

"You wear blinds, grandma, so you actually don't see anything that's not directly before your nose," Matt replied.

"The children love each other, Rebecca," Marjorie intervened. "Leave them be," she urged her.

"You're stupid, Marjorie," Rebecca lashed at her.

"You won't talk to my wife like this. I told you so in the past, and I won't repeat it again," Jonathan came to support his wife.

"I see," Rebecca said. "They fooled you all. They thought I'd hand in the money immediately if they came and gave me a teary story about love. I'm made of sterner stuff than that, Matty boy," she snickered at him.

"Maybe I wasn't clear," Matt repeated dryly. "I don't want the money. I already have here what I want," he said lifting Nora's hand.

"You know what I think?" Rebecca said with satisfaction. "I think you are afraid. If you weren't, you'd accept to have her checked by the trustees."

"She offered me her thoughts, so I know very well what she thinks and feels," Matt replied unconcerned. "I don't need your trustees to tell me what I already know," he shrugged.

Bryan put a hand on his shoulder, "Matt, in the long run, it helps that thing with the trustees. I've been there, done that, you know."

"I don't want them to read her mind," Matt dug his heels in the ground, glaring at Bryan.

"But I do," Nora replied calmly. "I know you know how I think, but maybe it's better if everyone is convinced that we don't try to pull the wool over their eyes," she told him, stroking his arm.

Matt closed his eyes in defeat.

FINAL CHAPTER

The sun shone over the island the day Nora married Matt. She wore a princess white dress, with little pearls all over the bust. The sleeveless dress hugged her bust and waist, but flared around her legs.

Nora had had some reservations at first. She'd been married before, after all, and it didn't seem right to wear a white dress.

But then, she'd discussed it with Marjorie, who, together with Becka, Lily and Maggie, insisted on going with her to buy the dress.

Her future mother-in-law patiently explained to her that she was wrong. Nora hadn't had a white dress for her first marriage. She'd married at the Town Hall. Besides, that was Matt's first and only marriage, and he'd love to have his bride dressed all in white.

Matt's eyes shone with unshed tears when she started moseying to him. His eyes roamed all over her face and body. Pride flashed in his dark-blue pupils.

He surveyed her advancement toward him, but, for the first time in his life, Matt lost his patience.

He dashed down the aisle, Marjorie had fashioned throwing a white carpet between the row of chairs. He didn't stop until he reached her, entwined his fingers with hers, and kissed her lips lightly.

"What are you doing, Matt?" Nora whispered, and her wide, bemused eyes zeroed in on his face.

"I made a mistake, baby. We should have had this ceremony in our living-room, under five minutes flat, and then leave for our honeymoon immediately. I don't know if I have the patience to go through all this. I want to be alone with you right now," he whispered back, and for the first time since her accident, he didn't think of the wound in her leg, but urged her to hurry and get before the pastor faster.

His action shocked everyone and they couldn't react at first. Marjorie covered her mouth and tears trailed down her face.

Becka and Bryan looked at each other, Becka taken aback, but Bryan with a wide and knowing smile on his lips.

Nat, who'd been told what was going to happen, didn't understand what changed and kept asking his aunties, "What's going on?" Yet, no one was able to give him an answer.

When Matt slid his arm around Nora's waist and rushed her before the pastor, they recovered and burst into laughter.

Jay and Maggie high-fived each other, as they were known to do, and the others elbowed one another. Even the old generation chuckled.

"He's got it worse than I had," Jonathan whispered to Marjorie, and she nodded, a smile on her lips, despite her tears.

Nora blushed to the tip of her ears, but Matt had only one care in the world. He simply wanted to get married and be on his way to the cottage he'd rented on the shore of a lake in north Ontario.

They'd already arranged and discussed things with Nat, and the child had declared he'd be happy to live with Becka and Bryan for a couple of weeks, while his mommy and Matt enjoyed a brief honeymoon.

Everyone enjoyed the brief service – Matt's stipulation, because he didn't want to waste the time before the *I do's.*

Rebecca had been invited as result to extensive interventions from all the women in the family and, especially, because of Nora's constant lobbying. Matt had turned ice-cold toward her and didn't want to talk or see her.

The engagement party had ended with inviting Rebecca's trustees so they could ascertain whether the young couple was really in love.

Matt had been completely against that, but Nora, who didn't want to be the cause of any discussions between Matt and his family, had insisted.

When the trustees acknowledged Nora and Matt's love and commitment, Rebecca had felt like fainting. She'd been wrong once more.

She'd tried to approach Matt, but he didn't bother to discuss anything with her. He just announced the trustees he didn't want or need the money, and then, he gathered Nora and Nat, said their good-byes and left.

Rebecca watched the couple making their vows and a shadow crossed her face. She knew Matt and she knew it wouldn't be as easy to get back in his graces as it had been with Bryan.

Matt was a kind man, yet he wasn't given to forgiveness. He'd already told her in unequivocal terms to stuff her money where the sun didn't shine. Nora had supported his decision, although she asked him to express it in more polite terms.

Some of the family members still talked to her, but not all of them. She didn't really need their pity, but that fiasco had decided her to find another way to get what she wanted.

Her eyes fell on Ariel, who tried to fight off the insistent invitations of Bryan's friend, Max. Rebecca shuddered. That was a man she didn't want in her family. Thank God, that girl seemed to have brains!

218

AUTHOR'S BIO

Rowena Dawn writes romance, reads thrillers and watches comedies. She likes walking through the woods, but insanely loves the sea. She has a love - hate relationship with her writing and drives her dog crazy whenever she doesn't stop writing to take him out.

OTHER BOOKS BY ROWENA DAWN

Becka's Awakening – Book One in the Winstons series

Jay's Salvation – Book Three in the Winstons Series (forthcoming)

Ariel's Dream – Book Four in the Winstons Series (forthcoming)

Leap of Faith

Double-Edged – Book One in the Perfect Halves Series

Eyes in the Dark – Book Two in the Perfect Halves Series

Pulled In – Book Three in the Perfect Halves Series (forthcoming)

Mr. (Almost) Right

Thank you for taking the time to read **Matt's Dilemma**, the second book in the series **The Winstons**.

If you enjoyed it, please, consider telling your friends or posting a short review.

Word of mouth is an author's best friend and much appreciated. Thank you,

Rowena Dawn

Contents

www.ingramcontent.com/pod-product-compliance
Lightning Source LLC
Chambersburg PA
CBHW070459200726
48293CB00007B/2298